W9-AVZ-222

The Masked Demon

a novella by

Mark Spencer

MINT HILL BOOKS
MAIN STREET RAG PUBLISHING COMPANY
CHARLOTTE, NORTH CAROLINA

Copyright © 2012 Mark Spencer

Cover design by M. Scott Douglass using a photo supplied by iStockPhoto.com

Acknowledgements:

Excerpts of this book have appeared in the following magazines:
> *Chelsea Hotel*
> *Florida Review*
> *Half Tones to Jubilee*
> *Westview*

Library of Congress Control Number: 2012944325

ISBN: 978-1-59948-374-0

Produced in the United States of America

Mint Hill Books
PO Box 690100
Charlotte, NC 28227
www.MainStreetRag.com

For Rebecca

CONTENTS

ONE

LARRY, CURLY, AND MOE

Oklahoma City, Oklahoma, 1962

Samson is lying on his back in the sun like a white whale beached on the patch of grass beside his and Darlene's trailer home, trying not to think about the fight he and Darlene had before he came outside to sun bathe, trying instead to imagine being a movie actor.

"The gods are pleased, Hercules," he says aloud to the white sky, trying to sound like Sir Lawrence Olivier.

Buddy Hoffman, the chief promoter of The World Wrestling Association since Stan Edwards died last year, has Hollywood connections. Jake The Snake (the son of bitch), Boyd "Bad Boy" Watkins, and Hammer Hamilton all got bit parts in the latest Hercules flick because of Hoffman, who left Samson a message yesterday at the arena in Muskogee, saying he wanted a private meeting with him in Dallas, and Samson figures—he hopes—it has something to do with him being in a movie.

But he's worried, too, because other private meetings with Hoffman have been bad. In the past year, Hoffman has made Samson do a new act in most of the cities on his circuit, be somebody else completely—The Masked Demon.

Samson's hope is based largely on the rumor he heard in San Angelo from The Grim Reaper that Hoffman is interviewing wrestlers he can lend to a Three Stooges movie in need of a lot of bodybuilders and strong men, a movie about The Stooges traveling back to the time of the Greek gods. If he has any lines to speak in the film, Samson wants to be impressive: "The gods are pleased, Larry, Curly, and Moe."

"Oh, shut up!" Darlene says from inside the trailer.

Then he hears the screen door squeak, opens his eyes, and is blinded by the fierce Oklahoma sun. He lifts his head and distressfully notes (not for the first time) that he can't see his feet for his belly; he remembers vividly when he looked like Mr. America. He suddenly doubts that Hoffman wants to help him get into a movie about Greeks and their gods. It's more likely that he'd play a blobby monster.

"Darlene, honey?" he says.

A shadow falls over him. He begins to turn his head, and this is when it suddenly rains two gallons of Dr Pepper that Darlene has poured from bottles into a tin bucket she usually fills with hot water and Spic 'n Span.

"Oh, honey. I deserve it. I know I do." The screen door slams. The lock clicks. Samson gets up and wipes his face with the red beach towel he was lying on. "Now, honey, let me in there. I gotta wash this stuff off. Good lord, sugar," and he laughs, "the fire ants will probably attack me and eat me alive."

For a minute, the space behind the screen door is gray like a gloomy morning but then fills with the colors of Darlene. She is six feet three inches tall and weighs a hundred and eighty-seven pounds, a great big pink beautiful woman with orange hair and green eyes in lime green shorts and a red and white striped blouse about to burst with her breasts. Samson has heard that Hollywood actresses wear steel-reinforced bras to make their boobs look like torpedoes or the pointed protrusions on the front bumper of a '58 Cadillac. Darlene needs no steel reinforcements. She is a miracle of nature.

"I hope them ants start with your pecker."

"Now, honey, watch what you say. The neighbors will hear you. And Tina Lee, too. Where is Tina Lee? Did she hear you say that word?"

"She's sleepin'. She can't hear, and she's too little to understand anyway. Peckerpeckerpecker."

"For God's sake, Darlene."

"I hope them fire ants chew up your balls and spit 'em out."

"Honey." Samson winces and squeezes his knees together. He looks around at the mobile homes nearby. In the one next to his and Darlene's, an old rusty beige one with no shutters or skirt around the bottom to hide the weeds and concrete blocks, lives the nosiest and ugliest woman Samson has ever known—uglier than even poor Jean Anne, his twin sister, who lives with their mama still and will never get married, no way.

The neighbor is a pile of lumps: two lumps for calves, two for thighs, a huge undulating one for a butt, another lump for a torso, and disproportionately small ones for breasts and a head. Every time he steps outside, Samson sees her gray face pressed at one of her window screens, her stringy, mousy hair done up in two pigtails like a young girl's, although she must be at least as old as he is, forty-three.

He fears that this hideous woman, who surely has never had a man, must be craving him, and when he has this thought, blurry images appear in his mind, and he shudders the way he does when The Harvard Horror (a guy who wrestles wearing a prep-school uniform and thick black-rimmed glasses) puts a Boston Crab Leg hold on him and Samson is supposed to experience pain no one in the arena or watching at home can imagine.

Darlene says, "I still don't know why you have to leave tonight."

Samson lets his eyes wander over their mobile home, one of the nicest in the park (Darlene should be more grateful, he thinks)—nice fake shutters on the windows, a fake chimney on the roof, and a really pretty fake fireplace inside, beautiful simulated walnut particle-board paneling in their bedroom. "I told you, honey, I'm sorry, but I got to be in Dallas in the mornin' to see that promoter Hoffman." The lie comes out smooth, slippery as a greased pig. He doesn't see Hoffman until tomorrow afternoon. "It's real important. Don't you want me to be a movie star?"

"Can't you change the time? See him later in the day so you can be with your family for a change?"

"Darlene, you're bein' unreasonable now. I'm tryin' to make a livin'. This is the way you was with Tina Lee, too." He looks at the section of the door behind which Darlene's belly is hidden, where a new baby is growing. He has noticed that her belly already gently swells out from her ribs.

Just yesterday they found out for sure. Samson sat in the waiting room of the OB's office, nervous as he was when he first started performing with The Baldwin Circus and Carnival back in 1936. Across from him at a desk was a cute little nurse, nut brown from the sun, who kept smiling at him because she had a good idea he was going to be a daddy again—everybody likes soon-to-be daddies, as if they must be naturally nice people if God would give them a little baby. Or maybe she was smiling because she got turned on looking at a man so big and powerful, a TV celebrity in the flesh, a former world-champion athlete—well, professional wrestler.

When the nurse got up from her desk and turned her back to slip a file into a cabinet, Samson studied her, tried to picture her wearing a two-piece bathing suit and working on that tan, tried to imagine the exciting contrast between her tanned parts and the parts that never saw the sun.

But, God, she was young enough to be his daughter. Just flirting would be a sin, especially under the circumstances, his big beautiful wife he loved so much getting checked to see whether her being sick and bitchy was because she was pregnant.

Still, Samson admired the nurse's tan, kept thinking about pale flesh that never saw the sun, and realized how much the little woman, only about five feet tall with dark hair long down her back, looked like Candy, the reason he's leaving for Dallas tonight instead of in the morning.

"Darlene, honey, let me in now."

Flies are gathering on his head and shoulders. Slapping at them, he walks up the three wooden steps and stands with his nose pressed into the screen. "Please, honey."

TWO

THE GODDESS OF SWEET SIN

Finally, Darlene breaks down, flips up the lock and lets Samson in, but she escapes from him before he can hug her and make up. She hurries down the hall—moves fast (surprisingly graceful for a big woman) the way she did when she was Darla The Devil Woman, The Goddess of Sweet Sin. She slams their bedroom door behind her. The lock clicks.

Just like a goddamn child, Samson thinks. Crazy when she's pregnant. For a moment he holds his breath as he glares at the bedroom door—a flimsy hollow thing he could easily reduce to splinters—before he goes into the bathroom, a tiny pink room almost like a closet for Samson, who weighs two hundred and eighty-eight pounds.

He wedges himself sideways between the sink and the linen closet. He pushes down his bathing trunks and sees no difference between the color of his hips and the rest of himself. He has a white fish belly of a body covered with swirls of black hair, some of it turning gray. He wanted some tan for his Texas Cage Death Match in three days because he will be wearing his Samson The Strong Man outfit, which shows a lot of flesh.

Samson looks at his face in the mirror above the sink. Big bags under his eyes are like miniature pot bellies. He lifts the hair away from his right ear. Above the canal, the ear is ragged and purple, a good half inch missing. Thanks to Jake The Snake. It's a wonder the fool didn't cut his whole damn head off, Samson thinks. Shrub shears. Christ.

He smoothes the hair back over his ear, looks at his shoulders. It seems that his shoulders get shaggier as the bald spot on the top of his head spreads. When the hair he tries to keep combed over the bald spot falls to the side, he looks like a monk, like Monk Morgan, who wears a friar's robe and sprinkles holy water that burns like acid in the eyes of evil opponents.

Samson reaches into the medicine cabinet for a green bottle of clear liquid he saw advertised in the back of *Goliath* magazine, the official journal of The World Wrestling Association. The label says that extreme caution must be taken in the use of the "tonic" because it promotes hair growth on any surface it comes into contact with. He imagines clumps of hair on his palms, on the end of his nose because he had an itch, on the end of his pecker ... .

He doesn't now because he would only wash it off in the shower, but when he does use it, he carefully pours a small amount onto a pad of cloth and dabs it gingerly on his bald spot. "This stuff don't work. Don't work at all. Fake as hell," he mutters as he dabs, but he keeps on dabbing and always washes his hands thoroughly.

And although the stuff has done nothing since he started using it three months ago, he still fantasizes about having thick wavy hair like Bobby Shine, the poor dead bastard who could have been world champion, had everything going for him, got laid more than movie stars; in fact, old Stan Edwards back in '54 was trying to link Bobby with Hollywood by starting the rumor that he was dating Grace Kelly. After Bobby died, she had to settle for the Prince of Monaco.

"You should of never let yourself get caught," Samson says to Shine's ghost. "More than one woman in the same city is dangerous."

Samson carefully slides sideways into the shower, pulls the plastic curtain closed, turns on the water, and lets the spray smack him in the face. He deserves it. A minute after he steps in, Darlene rips back the shower curtain and startles him. He drops the soap. She giggles at his high-pitched squeal.

He feels silly. Who did he expect? For a split second, a maniac. Like in *Psycho*. Janet Leigh. Nice hooters, Janet Leigh. Steel-reinforced bra? You could almost see them in that shower scene. But they aren't as nice as Darlene's.

Darlene is naked. Rosy pink, not white like him. Pink with a big triangle of orange pubic hair, the thickest bush he can imagine. As she steps into the shower, he lifts his arms to take her in, and she stoops, like a shy child, snuggling her face in his graying chest hair. He kisses the top of her head and pats her soft, fleshy back with one hand, the fingers of the other pressing into a cheek of her broad butt.

"I'm sorry," she says. "I know you work hard for us."

He kisses her head again.

She stands straight, and they are nose to nose. He looks into her eyes and sees his own. The water beats down on his back. They kiss. He leans her against the back wall of the shower and asks her to help him a little with her hand (he's an old man, after all, he jokes). Then he's on his way and pictures the trailer rocking with their weight and motion. It could topple over onto its side, and he wouldn't care.

Nibbling her neck. Fondling her breasts, which hang heavy, low as her belly button. They are incredible.

The water is cold by the time they're done. Darlene's face is rosy, satisfied. Samson is happy but suddenly hit by exhaustion. He maneuvers around to turn off the water, and they hear Tina Lee crying.

THREE

MIRRORS

In the dining area, a corner of the living room just off from the kitchenette, Samson sits across from Tina Lee, who's in her high chair. He feeds her apple sauce and creamed spinach that looks like something somebody already ate and couldn't keep down, while at the counter near the stove Darlene in a green and red plaid apron works fixing supper. She grinds up hunks of beef for hamburger in a grinder bolted to the counter. The muscles of her forearm ripple. In her sweet voice, she softly sings "Mac The Knife." She breaks off suddenly. "Sam, we're gonna need more room now that another baby's comin'."

Tina Lee won't swallow any more of the creamed spinach. Gobs of it slide off her bottom lip and down her chin. Samson says to her, "I don't blame you." She just wants the applesauce.

"Did you hear me, Sam?"

"Yeah, honey."

"Well?"

"Maybe we can get a trailer with three bedrooms," he says.

He remembers seeing one that had mirrors all along a wall of the master bedroom and red wallpaper with silver Cupids (chubby little creatures that remind him of the midget wrestlers). Mirrors would be nice.

Then he pauses with Tina Lee's tiny spoon in mid air. The baby strains toward the applesauce it holds, but he doesn't notice. It just hit him that the decor he imagined for a new mobile home might not be such a good idea; it might be a bad influence on his and Darlene's children, might corrupt them somehow. Be like growing up in a mobile whore house. He thinks of his boy Daryl Junior. Jesus, teen-agers. Teen-agers are crazy. Just watch them on "American Bandstand." Daryl Junior is sullen and lazy and crazy about rock 'n roll, and he's wrecked four cars in the five months since he turned sixteen.

Still nice, though—mirrors all along the wall. Then again Samson has gotten so fat it might not be much fun watching himself. In fact, at times lately, mirrors seem downright scary. At the rate he's going, he's afraid to think of how he'll look in five, ten years. Ten years—1972. Jesus. People will probably be driving bubble-top cars, like on "The Jetsons." Men will be on Mars. Kennedy will still be president, though—Candy would love to screw Kennedy, Samson would bet.

Lord, 1972. Darlene is only twenty-eight, so she'll be okay unless she lets herself go, but Samson will be fifty-three, and the way his belly is getting out of control, he has already seen the last of his pecker—need a mirror—although he keeps swearing to himself he'll go on a diet. He used to look like Mr. America. Mr. Universe. Fifty-inch chest, thirty-three-inch waist.

He looks out the back window that gives a view of flat, brown Oklahoma plain and a distant trash dump. By 1972 he might be dead.

Darlene is talking.

"Huh?" he says.

"I was sayin' I was thinkin' we could maybe buy a house. We should have plenty of money saved with the way you wrestle five or six nights every week. I do wish you'd let me know more about our money." She has her back to him, grinding meat. Now she turns to face him. "I don't mean to be morbid or nothin', but what if you was to die? I wouldn't know a thing."

She might find out plenty.

Death might be good. A way out. A flood of images fills his head. Bank figures. Accounts here in Oklahoma City, also in Dallas and Houston. Faces: Candy, Rachel Marie, Daryl Junior, Earl, Benny Bob, Mama, Jean Anne, Ray.

"Well, hon, maybe I'll make it big in the movies. You keep your fingers crossed for me."

Oh, Lord, he is a crazy son of a bitch, a bigamist. And he's supporting Candy, good as married to her but without the paper, which she is getting itchy for. *What if I got pregnant?* she keeps saying. Oh, Lord, not that. Three boys with Rachel Marie. Two babies now with Darlene.

Crazy. Mama would die of shame if she knew. Jean Anne would probably be happy as hell: she hates him. So does Ray.

FOUR

FOOD

Samson is quiet throughout supper. Darlene serves him four fat, greasy burgers on Wonder Bread with pickles and cheese and mayonnaise. As he eats the burgers, his fingers make wet impressions in the bread. He drinks buttermilk. He wipes his lips with the back of his hairy wrist, and Darlene tells him not to be a slob, to use his napkin.

Depression and fear always make him eat too much. Food compensates for the pain life doles out. That's why people eat a lot at funerals, he figures. He remembers eating the best chocolate cake of his life, a cake one of Mama's friends baked, the day Daddy was laid out at the Donie, Texas, Church of Christ. Being happy also makes him eat too much. When he's happy, he feels like celebrating with ribs, steaks, barbecue chicken, steer's brains, buffalo burgers, pecan pie....

"You look sad, Sam," Darlene says. "You sad 'bout something?"

He shakes his head, his cheeks stuffed with slightly burnt meat. He looks away from her, over at the grease-splattered stove, swallows, and says, "I was just thinking of my daddy. And I'm just... kinda wore out."

After supper, Tina Lee takes a nap in her crib back in her cubbyhole of a room, and Darlene sits on the sofa mesmerized by the big RCA TV that cost Samson a week's worth of wrestling matches. He bought it the same day he signed the lease on the little brick house in Dallas where he and Candy live. The old lady who owns the house and a bunch of others in worse neighborhoods Samson didn't want Candy living in asked him whether he and his daughter — Jesus, his daughter; is that what everybody thought? — were from Dallas or nearby.

Candy burst out laughing at the daughter part, loud and shrill, the only way she ever laughs, her perfect teeth flashing and her pink tongue glistening. But she didn't say a word and even walked away to hoot from a distance when Samson said, "My daughter and me are from Utah."

So all on the same day, he signed the lease, French kissed Candy good-bye, drove like a bat out of hell to Oklahoma City, went to a department store and bought the RCA TV in a maple-wood cabinet and presented it to Darlene as a surprise, as a way of saying he was sorry for something Darlene knew nothing about.

She laughs at something on "The Dick Van Dyke Show." Samson is at the table where they eat their meals. Scattered on it are plastic pieces of a model car. He likes to build models, to pour out onto a table the jumbled contents of a box, take that mess and make something nice: no glue showing, the rough edges filed down. Back in his and Darlene's bedroom are shelves holding the cars and airplanes and ships he's built: '37 Cord, '32 Cadillac, '48 Dodge, '38 Chevy, *The Spirit of St. Louis*, *The Bismarck*.

The model he's working on now is a '25 T-Model Ford. He had a real one in 1936 when he was seventeen (looked like Mr. Universe and thought for sure he'd be rich and famous some day), and he drove it all the way up to Wisconsin to join The Baldwin Circus and Carnival, where he fell in love with Macy, his first wife. She was a multitalented performer—a sword swallower and a lion tamer. Samson can't remember a happier time in his life than the four days they were engaged. The marriage, though, was a nightmare.

FIVE

SAMSON'S HEART

He was hoping to finish the T-Model Ford tonight, but he doesn't have time. He has to get ready to leave for Dallas. As he changes clothes, he sees the patches of pink sunburn that have started to hurt. He doesn't understand why the burn is uneven. There is a stripe of painful burn down the middle of his sloping belly and stripes on his arms and legs. His nose looks like a cherry. He looks, he thinks, like a barber's pole.

He puts his suitcase in the car, then goes back into the trailer to kiss Tina Lee and Darlene one more time. Outside, it's dark, the lightning bugs thick. Because he weighs two hundred and eighty-eight pounds—actually two hundred and ninety-one when he weighed himself on the scale in the bathroom after supper—he figures his heart has to be pretty big.

And as he holds up Tina Lee, rubbing his sore nose against hers, he feels that whole big heart swell with love. She has a clump of orange hair on top of her head but is still bald for the most part. She has green eyes and a little rabbit nose like Darlene's. Where are his genes? Maybe in the weak chin, the long earlobes. She weighs seventeen pounds now, but when she was born, she weighed only six. Darlene swelled up to a radiant two hundred and twenty-one pounds—he'd never seen such breasts in his life; she could have been a carnival act with those things—then that tiny kitten slipped out of her.

Tina Lee giggles at the nose rubbing. Then for no reason he can see, the little mouth stretches big and round, and two seconds later an ear-piercing wail erupts from it. Samson hugs her and rocks her and pats her and coos. He looks at Darlene for an explanation, for help.

"She knows her daddy's leavin' her again."

Amazed by what Darlene has said, amazed by the powers of perception of this tiny child, he looks at Tina Lee's scarlet face, holding her at arms' length now and squinting his eyes at her as if to get her in focus. He looks at Darlene again. Something sickening is happening in his heart.

"She's gonna miss her daddy."

It is as if a balloon full of blood has risen to his head and burst. He sees red. He drapes Tina Lee over his huge forearm and pulls back his right arm, his big paw hovering in the air, his palm tingling as if full of a swarm of bees, ready to cut the air and smack the baby's bottom. He is moaning, "Shut up, shut up," his hand trembling. Then the bees sting his palm as he smacks the thick diaper, and Tina Lee is wailing louder. "Oh, shut up. Please be quiet. Shut up. *Please!*"

Darlene grabs his arm and tries to hold it. "Sam, are you crazy? She's just a baby. You're just makin' it worse." Her big breasts jiggle; her hair, piled up on top of her head and pinned in place, quickly unravels and falls in her face splotched pink and red.

He realizes he's sweating like Jake The Snake, who's always as slick as a fish and smells worse. Everything Samson sees—Tina Lee, Darlene, the RCA TV—is blurred, and there are little explosions of light everywhere, stars popping and fading. The baby is screaming. Darlene is yelling nasty, muffled words. Bitchy. Bitchy when she is and is not pregnant. Goddamn woman doesn't appreciate this thick carpet or that TV or the rare, expensive pink-tone refrigerator. He loves her anyway.

She has Tina Lee, petting and kissing, then disappears down the hall toward the bedrooms. The stars are still exploding. Jesus, what is the matter with him? He rubs his eyes, wants to cry. Darlene returns without Tina Lee, calls him a crazy bastard, and attacks him with a heavy bronze ashtray she grasps easily in her big hand, putting welts on his forehead and the top of his skull before he can get out the door.

He storms out—tears the screen door off one of its hinges, thinks about turning the trailer over onto its side. But he just stands there in the dark, glaring at the pink and white trailer. Mosquitoes buzz around his head and around the light above the door. The light suddenly goes out.

The thumping of his heart fills his head. The roar is deafening like the hysteria of the crowd the night Jake The Snake snipped off his ear, like the rage of the fans the night The Fuhrer doused Samson The Strong Man with gasoline and took the world title from him.

From somewhere, barely piercing the racket in his brain, come the words, "Oh, God, the guilt." Finally, he runs up to the trailer, kicks a dent in its side, then flees.

SIX

CROSSING THE BORDER

In his brand-new 1962 Cadillac Eldorado, he cuts through the night at eighty-five miles an hour, whipping past slower cars and those giant trucks that usually scare him. He drives a hundred miles before he remembers to put on his glasses, which he's needed since he became nearsighted about five years ago. He plays with the electric windows, letting air rush in, then cutting it off. The radio wails country songs: Hank Williams, Johnny Cash, Conway Twitty, Loretta Lynn, Patsy Cline... Hank and Patsy can make him cry even when he's happy. Now Patsy catches him in a vulnerable moment—*crazy, crazy over you*—and his tears burst forth fat and salty.

He lifts his glasses and squeezes the bridge of his nose between thumb and forefinger, and the tears keep pouring down. The white Cadillac weaves. He grips the steering wheel with both hands. His foot eases up on the accelerator. He turns on the windshield wipers—a joke played on himself. But he can't laugh. He can't even smile. He can't see—the tears gush out.

Sweet Darlene.

A tractor trailer whooshes past him, doing ninety.

Good idea: steer into the path of one of those giant trucks. Solve all his problems in this world. A big crash, then a long drop to Hell. Land in burning embers. Brimstone. Get stuck with a pitch fork by the red-faced demon.

His destiny anyway, he figures. Why put it off?

But he would miss Darlene.

He thinks about the first time he saw her: in 1960 in the Stillwater, Oklahoma, High School gymnasium. He was the star of the evening (although he was supposed to lose), a former world champion scheduled to wrestle a new terror on the circuit, The Kansas Killer, as the main event after a ladies' cat fight.

The bleachers were half empty. Mean-looking, red-faced cowboys and young boys chewing tobacco were about the only people in the place. Stillwater was a college town— Oklahoma State University was there—but Samson didn't see any college students, except maybe for a couple of faggy-looking boys wearing fraternity pins on their sweaters.

College girls didn't come to see Samson the way they had gone to Bobby Shine matches. The same was true of the secretaries, school teachers, and nurses. Only Bobby Shine had been able to pull them into the arenas and gyms and VFW halls. The whole time Samson reigned as the king of The World Wrestling Association—World Champion in the Southwestern United States of America—he was aware that he was king only because Shine was dead. And if he managed to escape from Shine's ghost for a while and just enjoy the attention and money, a fan or a referee or another wrestler would make some remark to him like, "Guess *you* didn't cry too many tears at Bobby Shine's funeral." When somebody said that, Samson wanted to smash heads, draw some real blood. Shine was a legend with the advantage of being dead. Myth had it that he was the reason Marilyn Monroe and Joe DiMaggio broke up. In 1960, six years after Shine's murder, women were still visiting Shine's grave and leaving roses and their high-heel shoes.

A couple of nights before the match in Stillwater, as Samson made his entrance into the Dallas Gardens—the ring announcer introducing him as a truly great former world champion—a beautiful woman wearing diamonds and a mink jacket accosted him in the aisle. She sneered at him and said, "You're not half the man Bobby Shine was."

Samson was thinking about that woman as he wandered an empty hallway at Stillwater High School, the wall lined with lockers. He tried to open some of them, curious about what kids kept inside them, but they were all locked. He was thinking about how old he was getting to be (he had just turned forty-one), and he was sad about the recent death of Stan Edwards.

He went down to the gym from which boos and cheers and whistles were coming, and he peeked in at the ladies' match. The pretty one was decked out in what looked like a majorette's costume, tight and silver, her legs long and meaty. Her opponent was a three-hundred-pound nightmare who called herself Little Lil. She sat on Darla The Goddess of Sweet Sin, her blubber jiggling, and scratched at Darla's pretty face with her long blood-red fingernails.

Samson certainly did like the looks of Darla The Goddess of Sweet Sin, and he wanted her to notice *him*, to be attracted to him.

During his bout with The Kansas Killer he saw her standing in one of the doorways of the gym. Samson held The Killer in a head lock a long time so that he could look at her. She had cleaned the blood off her face and gotten dressed. She wore a fuzzy pink sweater and white slacks. Her luscious orange hair shone.

The Killer muttered, "Let me go now." Samson held on. "You're supposed to let me go." Samson tightened his grip. "Hey—"

"Oh, shut up." And Samson raked The Killer's eyes with his fingers.

"You got... to let... me go."

Samson looked at the top of The Killer's head. The Killer had dirty black hair full of dandruff. Samson tightened his grip even more.

The Killer let out a groan, began to struggle seriously.

Samson knew he'd get into trouble. The new chief promoter, Buddy Hoffman, wouldn't pay him for the match and would probably spout legal phrases like "breach of contract." But Samson didn't care. A wildness had taken hold of him.

The Killer whined, "I'm... supposed... to win."

But Samson flipped him over onto his back and pinned him. The referee hesitated.

"Count!" Samson yelled.

The ref slapped the mat.

Samson released The Killer, climbed over the ropes of the make-shift ring built on the center of the basketball court, and ran over to Darla, who was startled bug-eyed. "You wanta go out somewhere? I sure would like to get to know you, ma'am."

At first she had taken a step back but smiled now and stepped closer to him. In her high heels she was taller than he was. Her fingers and ears and wrists and neck glittered with glass jewelry. "I know a good place for a drink," she said.

They had to drive north for an hour to cross over into Kansas because Oklahoma was a dry state. Darla—"Darlene, actually," she told him—caressed the upholstery of his Cadillac and said, "You're only the second world champion I ever met."

"I'm just a regular person," he said. It didn't occur to him to tell her his real name. Almost no one had called him Daryl Lee in twenty years, except Mama and Rachel Marie. He'd never cheated on Rachel Marie; she was the mama of his three boys, and he'd known the pain of being cheated on.

"I met The Sheik about three years ago," Darlene said. "His cousins have a big pig farm in the same county where my mama's place is in Arkansas. Mama loves wrestlin'. She goes into Little Rock every chance she gets, and it's on TV every Sunday morning where she lives. Anyway, The Sheik's a real comical man. He knows a million jokes. Some are real dirty. And he can make real loud fartin' noises with his hand in his arm pit. He does that in restaurants sometimes and clears places out. People start makin' faces and then head for the door. Whole crowds pushin' to get out the door fast as they can. He's doin' a hillbilly comedy routine now up at Ozark Land Lodge."

"The fans really hated his guts, I can tell you."

"Yeah, he told me he'd been shot at twenty-six times."

"I never heard *that*."

"He might of just been tryin' to impress me. He wanted to add me to his harem."

Samson stared at her a moment, then returned his eyes to the dark road, waiting to hear more, wondering whether she was a whore.

She squirmed a little, then finally said, "I told him he was barkin' round the wrong bush. You know those eight girls that pretended to be his wives? They're all his first cousins. I think it's kinda of sick."

"He had the title just before me. He's the one I took it from."

"I remember that. That was about the time Bobby Shine got shot by some actress."

Samson's gut clenched. The landscape along the road was flat, treeless, black. "Yeah. But it was a stripper shot him. Not a actress."

"Yeah? Well, anyway, you know somebody really loves you when they shoot you."

"I reckon."

"Mama loved Bobby Shine. She'd bounce on the sofa like a kid when he was on on Sunday mornings. My pa got killed in the war in 1942, and I think the lack of you-know-what was startin' to wear on Mama some."

Samson cleared his throat. "Yeah, all the ladies liked him."

"I personally thought he was too pretty. Had a kind of baby face. Besides, that kind of man treats women real bad. Cheats and lies. Give me a rugged man, I say."

Samson looked at her. She smiled at him, her face softly lit by the dashboard lights. He grinned the rest of the way to Kansas.

They sat in a bar full of cowboys and under-aged kids just across the state line.

Samson said, "I was married once. It was when I was with a circus." Darlene's incredible breasts, covered by her fuzzy pink sweater, were actually *lying* on the table. "That was back in thirty-six, thirty-seven." Darlene's green eyes sparkled as she sipped her Bloody Mary. "I was the strong man. I bent iron bars. I juggled cannon balls. I lifted five hundred pounds with my teeth. It was all real, too. Nothin' phony. I got dentures now, I got to tell you. And... well... I only got a half of a left ear since 'bout a year ago." He self-consciously reached up and smoothed the long hair on the left side of his head. "You don't wanta see it. But I think honesty's important. That's why I'm tellin' you these things. Anyway, my marriage didn't last long."

"Was your wife in the circus?" Darlene had already told him how she waited tables in Tulsa for a year out of high school, then got discovered by a wrestling promoter she served donuts to. Just like a Hollywood story, she thought at the time, but now her back was giving her trouble, and most of the women she had to wrestle were pigs and lesbians.

Samson said, "My wife swallowed swords and did tricks with lions."

"What she look like? Was she pretty?"

"Oh, yeah. She was real beautiful. Or I thought so at that time. I don't know. She was okay lookin', I guess."

"Those circus girls are always pretty doll-like things. Little."

"I like big women myself," he blurted out, not able to take his eyes off her immense breasts. "I mean, I don't know. It was real sad for me. She wasn't what I thought she was. I thought she was a nice girl. I liked her daddy a lot. He was a fire eater. Nicest man I ever met except for my own daddy and Stan Edwards. Me and her had a real fast courtship. Knew each other two weeks, then got married in some town in Minnesota by a justice of the peace. A bald old guy that read the ceremony real slow." Samson smiled, remembering. "A couple of dwarves were our witnesses." He paused, frowned. "Then before we'd been married a week, these boys with the circus start winkin' at me and sayin' things like don't you just love the way she does this and the way she does that, like they all know exactly how she did this and that. A trapeze artist was the worse one for the talkin'. Then one day these Siamese twin boys start askin' me how I like the way she does this and that and a couple of things I'd never heard of. Siamese twins, for God's sake. Boys joined at the hips. And she keeps tellin' me all the boys are just jealous 'cause they'd been after her and I got her. But I didn't know if to believe her 'cause she'd lied about being a real blonde—"

Darlene raised an eyebrow, grinned.

He felt himself blush. "I'm sorry. I shouldn't be talkin' like this. My mama always taught me—"

"So what happened? Between you and your wife."

Samson shrugged. His heart filled with old love and sorrow. "I caught her in bed with a clown."

Darlene stared at him. Her face flushed. Her lips trembled. Then she burst out laughing. Samson waited while she cackled on for about five minutes. Anger swelled in the pit of his gut, pressed against his lungs and heart, made his chest hurt. He tapped his fingers on the table. He was getting a headache. "I'm sorry, sugar," she finally said. "What you do?" Then she laughed some more.

Samson had broken six of the clown's ribs and his pretty young wife's nose, but he took a long, deep breath and said to Darlene, "I just broke down and cried. I quit the circus the next day."

"That's sad." Then she hooted a couple of more times. "I'm sorry, Sam, but I keep seein' in my head some clown with blue hair and a big red nose and all."

Samson started to get mad.

But Darlene said, "Your wife must of been a fool."

"Why you say that?"

She looked down at her Bloody Mary, acted shy. "You're a handsome man. The real rugged type. But sensitive, too. Real nice." She reached across the table, touched his hand.

As Samson remembers this, driving toward Dallas and Candy, he can almost believe that Darlene really did think he was handsome. Then. Two years ago he was thirty-five pounds lighter and had a lot more hair.

Another giant truck roars past his Cadillac.

Death is not the answer. He would miss Darlene. He would miss them all: Darlene, Candy, Rachel Marie. And they would miss him, too, he's certain.

SEVEN

THE MUSIC OF ANGELS

Samson pulls off the highway and gets out of his Cadillac. He stretches and flexes. It's after three in the morning, and the sky is full of stars. The moon is full. The Cadillac's engine ticks, cools. Samson walks down the road to get his blood flowing. No cars pass. The silence is nice. His brother, Ray, used to say that silence was the music of angels. Ray used to be a preacher. Now he's a professional bowler.

Samson thinks of how he could just not go to Candy's. He could just stay away forever. His life would be one woman simpler. If she came to a match in Dallas, he'd ignore her. He could write her a letter saying he had found someone else.

But that would break her heart, and he loves her.

In the distance, a dog howls for a minute, then stops. Peace again. Samson looks up and sees a falling star. He remembers when he and his sister saw one. They were seven years old, and Jean Anne told him that it was a space ship full of Martians coming to take over the planet and barbecue all the humans. She said, "You know how you like steer brains? Well, the Martians just love people brains. They don't even cook them. They just split your head open and eat your brain raw with a fork."

Jean Anne was always scaring him with stories; she liked to because she thought he was stupid. They were twins, but her grades in school were a lot better than his. Ray was smart, too.

Ray and Jean Anne both hold a grudge against him now because they feel they should have been the successful ones in the family instead of him. They just haven't had much luck, Samson supposes. When he was a kid, he had common sense enough, but when it came to talents that stood out, he was best at lifting feed sacks and concrete blocks at his daddy's hardware store. Jean Anne and Ray won writing contests, spelling bees, Bible quizzes, and math competitions. Daddy used to say, "It's better to be lucky than it is to be smart."

And he was right. Samson has been lucky to find three wonderful women to love, to find a profession he's good at, to have Bobby Shine get shot dead... .

People still talk about Bobby Shine—*all the time.* Samson has tried to make peace with his ghost, but it isn't easy. *Goliath* magazine recently did a cover story called "What If Bobby Shine Had Lived?" Samson figures Shine would be blind and crippled from some venereal disease and a fat alcoholic (Shine was known to drink whiskey with his scrambled eggs every morning), but the magazine story claimed that he'd be in his eighth year as reigning world champion, that he'd be married to Grace Kelly or Marilyn Monroe, that he'd be making movies with Rock Hudson and Doris Day.

Samson's reign as world champion was short, under a year. The fans had loved to hate The Sheik. They had loved to love Bobby Shine. They liked Samson, but Stan Edwards said their "fire" for him was not hot enough. In 1955, Edwards was grooming a new boy on the circuit out of New Mexico who called himself The Fuhrer. He had swastikas tattooed on his arms and forehead and spoke in a thick German accent about the supreme race; he gave Nazi salutes and clicked the heels of his storm-trooper boots to

TV announcers, his opponents, and the crowds. The Fuhrer got to be champion for three years. Some of the fans even liked him. He had big fan clubs in Houston and Wichita Falls. Fights frequently broke out in the audiences between World War Two veterans and guys with swastikas drawn on their foreheads.

The Fuhrer held the title for three years. Three years. And Samson had it for only ten months.

Overall, though, he feels he's been one lucky son of bitch. His life could be better, but it could be a lot worse, and he wishes it weren't passing by so fast. His daddy died at forty-seven. Heart attack. One minute he was loading two-hundred-pound feed sacks onto a rancher's truck; the next, he was lying in the red dust, dead. Samson is only four years away from forty-seven. Four years is almost no time at all. He looks up at the stars, listens to the music of angels.

He turns around and heads back to the car. "The gods are pleased, Larry, Curly, and Moe," he says to the night. In about thirteen hours, he will be in Hoffman's office. *I can get you a big part in this movie called* The Blob. *You'll be the blob.*

Samson looks for another falling star, wonders whether he will ever see another one before he dies. He smiles, thinking of Martians eating raw human brains with forks. Martians carrying salt and pepper shakers around with them in their pockets. He loves Jean Anne and wishes she were not jealous of him.

When he was in high school, a pregnant girl who had screwed every boy over twelve in the town of Donie, Texas, claimed she'd been raped by a Martian. Tammy Sue White gave a date and a time, said it happened in a cotton field on the edge of town, and she cried when she described the hideous alien with its red eyes and bald head and fat belly and its enormous lust.

Everybody whispered that it sounded a lot like a description of Elmer Appleton, the mayor.

Samson had humped Tammy Sue himself on six occasions on top of some feed sacks piled in the stock room of his daddy's hardware store.

Tammy Sue stuck to her Martian story and went off to Ardmore, Oklahoma, where she had cousins, to have the baby. She never came back to Donie. Rumor was she married some slightly retarded man who made cane chairs for a living. Samson heard years later that she had moved to Nebraska and that her son was a football star.

Over the years, Samson has sometimes wondered whether there's a half Martian somewhere in Nebraska that looks like him.

EIGHT

THE MUSIC OF CANDY

Dallas, Texas

Just as the sky turns pink in the east, Samson pulls into Candy's driveway. Weeds grow up from cracks. Trembling slightly from fatigue, he sits in his Cadillac and looks at the house. He thinks of all his homes as his women's homes, none as his own somehow, not even the one he shares with Rachel Marie, not since he started cheating on her. *The son of man has no place to rest his head,* he remembers from somewhere.

Candy's house is small and built out of ugly red bricks and surrounded by houses just as small and just as ugly, houses with tricycles out front and cars that all seem to have a smashed tail light. The ugly red bricks remind him of the faces of people who hate him when he wrestles as The Masked Demon.

Candy's yard has no shrubs, no trees, no flowers. The weedy grass has died from lack of rain and the searing Texas sun. Every time he drives up to this place he thinks about getting Candy a better house, but money is a problem.

Money from being in movies would really help. His meeting with Hoffman is only ten hours away.

Occasionally he thinks about not driving a Cadillac, getting a cheap Ford or Chevy instead, but he loves the Cadillac—its gleaming buxom chrome bumpers, long smooth milky-white lines, and flared tail fins. If it were a woman (he has told Candy), the sight of it would make him hard.

He rationalizes that the Cadillac is a necessity, although if he got rid of it he could maybe afford to get Candy a nicer place and Rachel Marie a dishwasher and Darlene a house instead of a trailer. The Cadillac, though, is part of an image—an image that Darlene married, that Candy shacked up with, and that Rachel Marie has grown used to in recent years. He is afraid that if he didn't have a new white Cadillac every year his women might not love him as much.

The porch light is on, yellow, and he thinks about the light on Darlene's trailer going out. He feels bad about acting crazy, but he's almost certain he and Darlene will make up, as always. Even on their wedding day in the Glorious Resurrection Baptist church in Devil's Elbow, Arkansas, they fought: Darlene had asked him to call the editors at *Goliath* magazine and have them send a reporter to the wedding to take pictures and write an article. She had never had anything written about her in *Goliath*; she said the headline could be "WRESTLERS WED." And their smiling faces could be framed by a heart. There could be a picture of her in her laced-trimmed, white satin wedding dress.

She was furious that a reporter hadn't shown up. At the reception at her mama's house she kept saying she was going to call the magazine and give the editors hell. Finally, Samson told her he'd forgotten to ever contact the magazine; it just slipped his mind. His silly brain was like a greased pig. Darlene's mouth dropped open, then clamped shut like a bear trap, and her eyes turned into black slits. She hurried away and locked herself in her old bedroom there at her mother's house, and when he tried to talk to her, she shouted through the door that she was going to get a divorce.

Now, getting out of his Cadillac takes great effort.
He groans. He thinks of having to wrestle tonight. He's
scheduled to be Bible Bob, an act he created a year ago and
talked Hoffman into letting him do in Dallas, if nowhere
else. He likes being Bible Bob, but he's so tired right now he
can't imagine being able to work tonight.

Candy's front door is unlocked. Unlocked for any rapist
who wants to walk in or any son of a bitch fat phony who
loves and is mean to too many women.

The living room walls are bare, cracked in places
although the house is only twelve years old. There are
a couple of brown rugs on the linoleum floor, a rocking
chair with a broken slat, a scarred-up coffee table, a sofa
with soda pop and milk stains all over it (Candy bought it
second-hand from people who had little kids), a TV on a
rusty metal stand. These are all things Candy had in a tiny
apartment in a bad section of Dallas thick with Mexicans
and Negroes.

Samson has told her that he's lived in motel rooms his
entire adult life and has given most of his money to a greedy
government and to a bunch of distant-but-very-needy
relatives, so she doesn't ask for much, and anyway, actually
thinks this little house is nice. Still, Samson has gotten her
a few things. One stands in a corner of the living room,
looking as out of place as his Cadillac would in a junk yard:
a thousand-dollar grandfather's clock.

Despite its shabbiness, the living room is clean and
straight. Candy has been demonstrating her housekeeping
skills, showing that she will make a good wife. She's been
cooking, too. In the kitchen is an apple pie, which Samson
pours a mound of sugar on top of. Then he scoops out a
hunk with his big paw. He eats standing next to the new
dishwasher.

When he has finished the entire pie, he licks his hand
and heads toward the bedroom. On the wall over the new
brass bed is a big iron crucifix that cost Samson a hundred

dollars. Candy wanted it badly. Samson didn't want it at all. It must weigh thirty pounds. There are dabs of red paint on Jesus' hands and feet, and Jesus sorrowfully looks down on the bed. Samson is afraid it will fall one night. It could crush his skull. Why Candy wants that dangerous Jesus to watch them fornicate he'll never understand. She's a Catholic; his mama warned him about Catholics, said they never missed church but took sinning lightly—would just confess their sins away instead of feeling guilty the way they should.

When Samson's brother was a preacher, Ray devised a point system to rate the severity of various sins and their consequences. Ray would get into arguments with lay people and other preachers at his bowling alley crusades or on the streets of Donie about things like whether cussing was worse than having lustful thoughts and about whether a sacrilegious curse like "Goddamn" should have a higher point value than a secular but more obscene one like "fuck."

Big brother Ray was preaching before Samson left home to join the circus, and Samson really admired him. He always wanted to know—but was too shy to ask—how many points Ray had assigned to masturbation.

Adultery was worth a couple of thousand points.

Candy's chest-of-drawers and nightstand are white, little-girl pieces of furniture, marked up and old, bought by Candy at a used-furniture store after she left home. Home was an unpainted shack, she told him, on a dried-up piece of what was supposed to be a farm in southwestern Texas. She never wanted to go back there.

Moonlight slants through the window, falling on Candy, making her dark flesh luminescent. She is spread out on her back in the heat, naked, her mouth open slightly, snoring softly. She is a vision. Samson takes off his clothes and eases into bed, not wanting to wake her, this prize he cannot believe he has won.

Then in his exhaustion, half asleep, he wonders what she does with her time. She used to be a sales girl at Sears, Roebuck, but he made her quit. She can't watch TV all day, can she? Make apple pies? Dust? Mop?

And maybe screw skinny-assed Mexicans right here in his brass bed?

No. He wants to trust her. He tries. He has no reason not to. Turning, he gently pats her arm, kisses a nipple.

But how can he believe that she would be true to a fat old man like him? She is barely twenty and has fine black hair like a full-blood Indian's, straight and shimmering all the way down to her tail bone. Her body, full of hot Spanish blood from her mama's side, is like a Las Vegas show girl's. She has the roundest, smoothest bottom he has ever seen.

She rolls onto her side and opens her eyes, black, and without a word, starts loving on him. As tired as he is, as full of worry and suspicion as he is, he finds himself making love enthusiastically. Slick and shiny with sweat now, she moves and groans under him. Clutching his hairy shoulders, she has a string of little firecracker orgasms, one every few seconds.

Jesus, he swears to himself as he always does in these moments, isn't this what men live for?

She whispers, "On top," and they turn so that she's above him. She leans her head down and brushes his belly with her long hair. Faster and faster she rides him, making husky sounds that remind him of when Rachel Marie was in labor with each of his boys.

Now Candy presses her face against his neck, and her noises become higher pitched, even shrill. The most beautiful music on earth.

Jesus, he will never go to the others again; he will give up wrestling, hide out, move to Utah—where the Mormons live—and build a log cabin on a mountain, raise some sheep, and screw his life away with Candy. His sunburn hurts, but the hell with that.

Then he comes so hard he thinks he'll surely have a stroke or heart attack.

Then slowing down.

Calm. Fatigue again.

Floating, wet all over. A chill.

Sleep.

NINE

MONSTERS

Sleeping beside Candy, one of her legs lying across his hairy thighs, he snores and dreams. First, he dreams of The Three Stooges. They're beating him up, kicking his shins, biting his nose, pulling his hair. Then Moe has shrub shears and is going for his good ear. Then Moe becomes Jake The Snake, and suddenly both of Samson's ears are flopping around like fish out of water in the garden behind his mama's house, alive and bloody, hopping between rows of tomatoes—until Buddy Hoffman materializes, rising up like a mutant corn stalk out of the cabbage patch, and stomps the ears with his black wing-tip shoe, grinding them into the dry, hard earth as if they were large bugs.

Samson shudders, is awake a moment, only a moment.

For a few seconds he dreams of screwing the little nut-brown nurse on the reception desk in Darlene's doctor's office.

Then he dreams that Rachel Marie is laid out in a coffin. In real life, she is skinny and frail as a granny. In the dream, the coffin is only about three inches wide, but it's big enough for her yellow corpse. Samson keeps asking everyone in the room—his mama's kitchen, the coffin on the table—what happened. His boys are here, his mama, Darlene, Candy, Jean Anne, Ray. Ray rolls a huge black bowling ball through the living room of Mama's house, and it crashes into the television set, which explodes and catches fire. He then turns to Samson and says, "Daryl Lee, it was her heart. Rachel Marie's heart just kept shrinkin' with the rest of her."

Samson wakes up crying.

Candy stirs, mumbles something he can't understand, then rolls onto him, hurting his sunburn. She kisses his tears and sleepily says, "What's wrong, you big ole thing? Is a monster gonna get ya?"

"I am the monster," he groans.

She reaches down, grabs his private parts, and mutters, "You sure is," and then is asleep again.

TEN

THE WAY YOU ARE

Samson manages to sleep through the morning but restlessly. He wakes up periodically, sweating. He pulls a pillow down over his face to hide from the light.

A little before one, he throws off the pillow and sits up. He hears Candy's soap operas on in the living room. While he showers and shaves, the television is louder so that she can hear it in the kitchen as she fixes him fried eggs, bacon, and waffles.

In this medicine cabinet, too, there is a bottle of the stuff that is supposed to grow hair on an apple. He dabs it on his head and then stares at himself in the mirror. A monster.

The hair on the top of his head is thinner than ever, while the long hair on the sides and back hangs limp to his shoulders, graying. Maybe, he thinks, he'll color it platinum or white, the color of the wig he wears when he wrestles as Bible Bob. He has kept his hair long because of his Samson The Strong Man act. Now it is being shorn—not by a beautiful Delilah, he tells himself—he always pictures Hedy LaMarr, who played Delilah in a movie a few years ago—but by that old bitch Age.

It's not just losing his hair that bothers him; it is also what's happening to his face. It's gotten puffy looking. And his skin is slack and splotchy. For twenty-five years, it's been scarred from teenage acne. When he locks the bathroom door and removes his dentures to clean them, he becomes an old, old man.

Wearing the white robe Candy gave him last Christmas— Lord, that was a mess, trying to spend some Christmas with each woman—he ambles into the kitchen, depressed. And standing by the table, watching Candy, who's wearing tight denim shorts and a red halter, work at the stove, he says, "I... I don't know why... why you love a fat ugly old man like me."

She puts down her spatula, turns, hugs him, and steps back to the stove, and says, "You're bein' silly when you say such things."

"I just don't see how you could. I ain't no Bobby Shine."

"Who?"

"*Who*? You don't know Bobby Shine?"

"He some actor?"

Samson smiles. "No." He sits down at the kitchen table, listens to the popping grease, a happy sound, inhales the smells of bacon, eggs, waffles, and coffee. Then without thinking about it, he says, "I'm gonna buy you a new stove! You go pick one out! Anything you want!"

Candy turns, looks at him, her mouth open. "General Electric?"

"General Electric. Westinghouse. Lincoln Continental. Hell, you get whatever kind you want." He realizes that she was only around eleven years old when that stripper stuck her pistol in Bobby Shine's ear. And she never reads the wrestling magazines. "A Cadillac stove," he says. "Does Rolls Royce make one?"

"Silly," she says, setting his food in front of him, steam rising into his face.

The four fried eyes are sunny-side up. Perfect. Big round yellow eye balls staring up at him. Martian eyes. He stabs the fuckers. "Thank ya, baby."

She starts wiping off the stove. "Hear what President Kennedy did?" she asks.

"President Kennedy?" The grease isn't popping any more. The eggs taste too salty. This interest of hers in politics is strange. She's a prize, but she's also a dumb country girl and a child. Of course the answer is that she has no real interest in politics—only in a pretty-boy dream man she probably fantasizes about when fat old men are on her.

She says something Samson doesn't listen to.

Anger and hurt rise from his heart into his throat. "Too bad you ain't old enough to vote." Bobby Shine. John Kennedy. Two of a kind. "But I bet you'd like to lay Kennedy, wouldn't you?"

"What? Sometimes you're crazy, Sammy."

"Man's younger than me and he's the goddamned president of the United States of America."

"He just looks young. He's actually two years older than you," she blurts out.

Samson glares. "Thanks."

"Oh, Sammy!"

"You know a lot 'bout him."

"Sammy." She stands with her hands on her hips and smiles down at him. "He ain't never been a world champion at nothin'," she says.

"Shhhiiiit," Samson drawls and ducks his head between his shoulders modestly.

"Let's talk about somethin' else." She sits down across from him. He looks at her deep cleavage. They're not big enough to have to lie on the table like Darlene's, but there's plenty. Sweet things. She is truly a prize. She notices the look on his face. "What you thinkin' about, you big ole thang?"

"Nothin'. I mean ... nothin'."

"Oh, come on."

"Well, I ... I was thinkin' about Jayne Mansfield."

"What about her?"

"I was thinkin' 'bout how much prettier *you* are."

"What about Marilyn Monroe? She's my favorite actress."

"You got her beat by miles."

"Wouldn't you like me better if I was blonde?"

"I like you the way you are."

"Sammy, let's get married."

"Huh?"

"Sometime soon."

"Now, hon, I don't know."

"Oh, come on, Sammy. Let's pick a day."

"I told you, honey, I don't know. I mean, not *now*. Me on the road all the time and... and all." He stuffs a waffle in his mouth and chews.

"What if I got pregnant?"

He chews for a long time, staring at the eggs on his plate. She waits. "You won't get—" he says. "I'm too old to get girls knocked up." He laughs, thinks of Darlene, takes a big bite of waffle and almost chokes. He feels sweat beads popping out all over his fat face.

She says, "But President Kennedy... Well, never mind."

"Maybe after I'm real rich and famous as a movie actor, we can." He believes that if he gets into movies he can handle anything. He can have a dozen wives.

"You're makin' me sad. I just want you to know that. I'm gonna go watch TV now."

She goes into the living room and stares at a soap opera. A little while later, he asks her to get him a Dr Pepper, and she does and even leans down to kiss his cheek before she goes back to her show. Not like Darlene. Candy doesn't sulk much or bitch or slam doors. More grown up in some ways. Or maybe she's just waiting to get the ring. Then *bam!*

He has an hour before he has to go see Buddy Hoffman. Candy is interested in her soap operas, so he goes to the hall closet, gets out a box, and pours the plastic contents onto the kitchen table. He's working on a '32 Packard.

ELEVEN

THE GODS ARE PLEASED—REJOICE!

The gods are pleased, Larry, Curly, and Moe," Samson says as he drives into downtown Dallas. He has classical music playing on the radio, although he doesn't like it. He has it on because it's the kind of music played in all the Biblical movies. He hopes to start his career in movies by working with The Three Stooges and then quickly move on to working with Steve Reeves in Hercules flicks and then with Charlton Heston in Bible films.

Maybe someday he will get paid to kiss Elizabeth Taylor. He wonders whether Bridgette Bardot is planning to do any Bible movies.

He feels good. Nervous but good. Movie actors make piles of money. He'll be better able to take care of his women. He has saved them and now must keep them safe. He wants to give them things that will make them happy; he wants to shelter them from evil, from danger, from men who wouldn't treat them well or love them as much as he does.

Samson is certain he's the best thing that could have ever happened to Darlene, to Candy, to Rachel Marie. Ray wanted to marry Rachel Marie; if he had, he would have made her miserable because now Ray's a bum. Samson loves his brother, but there's no denying what Ray has become since he gave up preaching.

Samson's children have a wonderful daddy. He feels sorry for any child who is not his. He feels sorry for any woman who is not his.

His Cadillac floats along the street, filled with violins, flutes, oboes, crashing cymbals. Samson is full of love for his women and his children and his mama and his brother and his sister. He wants to protect them all, make them all happy.

The gods are pleased.

Give him the world, and the world will rejoice.

TWELVE

THE WRITING ON THE WALL

Every time Samson sees Buddy Hoffman he'd love to piss on Hoffman's head, but today he needs to be careful not to show his dislike.

Samson feels lightheaded as he rises in the elevator to the ninth floor of this run-down building Hoffman has his office in. The building doesn't have air conditioning, and the hunchback dwarf who operates the elevator has on just a sleeveless tee shirt tucked into baggy pants with smears of beige paint all over them. Samson notices the dwarf has no socks on, and his big toes stick out of slits in his shoes.

The elevator creaks, ascends painfully slowly. The dwarf is perched on a high stool next to a lever. With what seems to be complete indifference, he stares at Samson. Samson stares through the iron gate. Each time they pass a floor, Samson can see a hallway with chewed-up carpet or buckling tiles and a row of darkly varnished doors. Sometimes there's the low tinkling of a record player. One time when he was on his way up to Hoffman's office, Samson glimpsed a bald woman wearing nothing but panties crossing the hall from one room to another. The day Hoffman told him he was to become The Masked Demon, Samson saw a man in a suit lying face down and motionless in the hall of the third floor; an hour later, when Samson was on his way down, the man was gone, and the hall was empty, all the doors closed as usual. The doors on all the floors are almost always closed. Some bear the names of businesses: "Lou's Loans," "American-Way Loans," "Wally's Imports," "Madame Sophie—Palms Read, Dogs Shampooed," "Paradise Construction." Some floors are made up of apartments rented by hookers and beatniks.

Between every floor, on the wall of the shaft, somebody has smeared the words "Fuck You" with beige paint.

The dwarf suddenly says, "Hey, Demon"—Samson is startled, jerks; he twists his head to look at the dwarf—"I hear a lady in Wichita Falls attacked you with a butcher knife."

Samson says, "Hat pin. Damn near put it through my head. Bobo Brazil grabbed her from behind just in time. One reason I don't care much for that Demon crap. Think I'll tell Hoffman I ain't doin' it no more."

"When I was World Midget Wrestling champion, a fat woman got in the ring one time, grabbed me and turned me upside down, holdin' my ankles, and spanked me." The dwarf grins. His teeth lean every which way like old tombstones and are black and yellow.

"You was a world champion?" Samson asks.

"Six years. Thirty-three to thirty-nine. I was a goddamn legend. Pete The Pint-Sized Punk, they called me. I don't look like much now, but I was the meanest little son of bitch you'd ever wanta fuck with. I'm not washed up either. Mr. Hoffman's gettin' me a part in a movie."

The elevator jerks to a stop. Samson asks, "What movie? You talkin' 'bout a Three Stooges?"

"Yeah. And after that Mr. Hoffman's gettin' me a part with Liz Taylor."

"He already told you you got the part in The Three Stooges thing?"

"Yeah. A month ago. What? You think I'm shittin' ya?"

"A month ago?"

"Yeah. I signed a goddamned contract. You can see it if you think I'm shittin' ya."

The dwarf hasn't opened the gate yet.

"You gonna let me outta here?"

"I was world champion six goddamn years."

"Yeah, I know."

"And I'll tell ya somethin' else. I gotta a mind to fuck Liz Taylor."

"You gonna let me out or you tryin' to kill me with your bad breath?"

"I might be short, but I'm hung like a horse. I've laid eight hundred and forty-seven dames in my life."

"Congratulations." Samson sighs, stares through the gate. Hoffman's office is at the other end of the hall. "WWA" is painted on the dark door.

The dwarf unlatches the gate, jerks it open fast, and Samson is barely out when the elevator begins its descent. Samson's heart is racing, and he's soaked in sweat. It must be a hundred degrees up here. *A month ago. Liz Taylor.* Samson's sweat drips to the dingy carpet.

When Samson opens the door, Hoffman's sitting at his gray metal desk and reading the newspaper. Hoffman has no secretary. "Sam. You're a bit late."

"Been in your elevator held captive by the dwarf for a week."

Hoffman laughs. "Pete's something, isn't he?"

"Yeah. I don't know what, though."

Hoffman rises from his chair and offers a hand dirty with ink and sweat. Samson holds his breath and makes the handshake short. "Sit, Sam. Sit."

Giving orders to him like he's a dog.

Hoffman has a fan on his desk positioned to blow on his face. Hoffman's face is fat and covered with acne scars. Every time he sees Hoffman, Samson worries that the two of them look a lot alike, could even be mistaken for brothers— *twin* brothers. His stomach churns hate whenever he thinks of how Hoffman has made him wrestle as The Masked Demon in almost every city on the circuit except Dallas and Houston. In Dallas, he gets to be Bible Bob. In Houston, he's still Samson The Strong Man. But everywhere else he's The Masked Demon. His stomach pukes the hate up into his head, making his head throb painfully.

"I want to talk to you about something really interesting, Sam." Hoffman leans forward, his elbows on his desk. Hoffman is Samson's age, a fat man, bald on top. He was a screenwriter and actor in Hollywood for twenty years, probably never doing anything any good; at least Samson never heard of him. "What I'm thinking of doing for you would mean more work, more time away from home, longer travel distances, but great career opportunities." Two things Samson has to hand the man, though: he has good taste in cars—a sky-blue Cadillac Eldorado—and in women—a young blonde wife with tits like melons; whenever Hoffman attends a match, she is always on his arm.

"I like to work," Samson says. "You know me. I'm real ambitious." Samson thinks about how he'll have to get The Three Stooges' autographs for his boys. Candy and Darlene, too. Rachel Marie thinks The Stooges are silly and too violent.

"I'm glad you feel that way, Sam." Hoffman leans back in his chair and looks around at the posters on the walls of some of the wrestlers currently on the Southwest circuit: Bobo Brazil, Iron Man Mike, Junk Yard Dog, Igor, The Beast, The Masked Demon." "Pro Wrestling is going to do nothing but get bigger. The kids just now getting into it are going to have it made." Hoffman nods toward one of the posters on the wall. "A kid like Iron Man Mike is going to be around a long time. Reminds me of Bobby Shine. A little."

"Yeah, I reckon. You sure do like havin' Mike clean The Demon's greens often enough."

"Demon's a great character, Sam. And you're good at bein' him."

"Bible Bob would be as interestin' a world champion as Iron Man Mike is."

"Bob's okay in Dallas, but the religious-hero theme is going to lose its appeal. Why, the government's going to stop letting kids pray in schools."

"But—"

"No, Sam." Hoffman swivels in his chair and looks out the window at the Dallas slums.

Samson decides not to pursue the issue now. "Can we maybe get on then with what you wanted to tell me?"

"Sure." Hoffman swivels to face him again. "It's this. How would you like to wrestle in Mexico?"

"Where?"

"Mexico."

"The country?"

"Yeah."

"You mean in movies?"

"What movies?" Hoffman says. "See, we're expanding into Mexico. We'll hold matches in a lot of border towns and in the bigger cities, too. Even Mexico City. Beautiful place. The natives and the tourists down there love wrestling, and we can do a lot of things there in the ring we can't here."

"Do things?"

"All kinds of things."

"Like what?"

"I'll explain that part later, Sam. I've got a lawyer looking into it."

What can the bastard mean? Samson wonders. They already do just about everything there is to do in the way of physical torture. Of course, it's fake. Maybe Hoffman means it won't be fake down there.

Real blood. Real broken backs. This son of a bitch wouldn't care as long as he gets his money—Samson has heard that regardless of this rat-hole of an office Hoffman is rich as God and lives in a mansion.

Maybe there would be something to do with perversion. Naked lady wrestlers? Maybe men, too? Something having to do with animals?

"What 'bout the Stooges movie?"

"What about it?"

"I thought you were gonna maybe get me a part in it."

"I can't do that."

"You got that goddamn dwarf a part!"

"You're just not right for any of the roles. You're too old, Sam. And I'm sorry to say this, but you're overweight."

"Ain't the dwarf too old and too short?"

"There're roles for dwarves. Listen, I'm just being frank here. And I'm telling you this Mexico thing is a real opportunity. Better than a movie. Who the hell wants to be in a Three Stooges movie?"

"I ain't doin' no crap in Mexico. I got a family I don't see enough as it is."

Hoffman leans forward again and places his palms flat on top of the desk. "Hear me out, Daryl," he says, using Samson's real name.

"I don't wanta hear." Samson knows this is the time to walk out, but Hoffman has a lot of power, and Samson knows if he goes too far he'll be lucky to get two bouts a week and he'd probably be wrestling nowhere but El Paso.

"Hey, it'll be fun, Daryl. Maybe we can work something out concerning money, a good deal for you, you being a vet after all of... of how many years?"

"Seventeen."

"Right. And a former world champion."

"More money, you say?"

"Sure."

"Now what exactly we gonna do down there if I agree?"

"Well, for one thing, I want you to be The Masked Demon exclusively."

"I'd never be Samson The Strong Man?"

"No."

"No Bible Bob? I bet the kids still pray in the schools down *there*."

"The tourists and the Mexicans will love The Masked Demon."

"What else? What are these things we can get away with you're talkin' 'bout?"

"We'll just be adding a few things. Not many. The act will be basically the same."

"Like what?"

"I can't go into it until I get some more information from the lawyers."

Samson leans his head to one side, squints his eyes at Hoffman. "You want me to screw pigs or somethin'?"

Hoffman laughs. "Now, Daryl, let's just drop it for now. I already talked to Berry Beaner by the way. And The Mad Hungarian. And Jake The Snake. Handsome Harry Kline. They're all willing and *eager* to wrestle down there."

"Those guys all screw pigs for a hobby."

Hoffman laughs again. When he stops, he says, "Trust me." The son of a bitch keeps smiling. His white shirt has giant sweat stains under the arms.

"But I *don't* trust you."

"Daryl, you're paranoid. Hey, you all set for tonight? I have to admit the Dallas crowds go for Bible Bob. In Mexico he'd be a flop. Everyone would just want to see him dead. A wrestling priest maybe but not Bible Bob. But they'll love The Demon."

"I ain't wrestlin' in Mexico. I got a contract says I don't have to travel no farther than Oklahoma or New Mexico, and it don't expire till 1965. I got a family I need to spend time with."

"I know you're a big family man, and I admire you for that. How is the family?"

"They're good."

"They're in Oklahoma City?"

"Yeah." Samson blinks fast three times, decides against correcting his mistake. His heart is suddenly beating harder than a scared rabbit's. He stares at Hoffman. He has always told Hoffman his wife and kids are in Houston. Does the son of a bitch know something?

"I'd like to meet the good woman some time when I'm down there."

"Did he emphasize the word "down"? He *knows*, Samson thinks. Oh, Lord, the son of a bitch knows.

"Tell you what, Daryl. The Mexican thing. No rush. Give me a call in a day or two, and we'll talk some more." Hoffman stands up, steps around his desk, and walks Samson to the door, patting Samson's sweat-soaked back. "Good luck tonight, Bob." Hoffman grins.

Samson can only nod. Instead of taking the elevator, he goes down to the end of the hall, climbs out the window, and takes the fire escape.

THIRTEEN

BIBLE BOB—KICKING BUTT FOR GOD

He tells Candy he got to Hoffman's office and Hoffman wasn't there.

"Ah, there was a note on the door." Samson drops down on the sofa.

"What it say?" Candy climbs onto his lap.

"Oh, it said somethin' 'bout a family emergency. That's all. So I didn't get to find out nothin' 'bout the Stooges movie."

"Maybe you'll see him tonight at the arena."

"Maybe. But... you know, I don't know anyway, baby. I been thinkin' how I'm just a simple good ole boy. I shouldn't be messin' in the movie business with a bunch of dope addicts and beatniks and wild women."

Candy studies him a minute. There's something sad in her eyes, but then she smiles. "You're probably right." The sad thing in her eyes is still there. "You're more the politician type anyway. Don't politicians make a lot of money, too?"

"What you sayin'? You want me to run for governor or somethin'?"

"It's an idea. You can't wrestle forever. You got thousands of fans, and I could campaign with you." Candy's voice rises with excitement. "I could be like Jackie Kennedy!"

"Have you lost your mind, girl?" Samson squirms. "You're sittin' on a bad place, baby."

Candy gets off his lap and drops down onto the other end of the sofa. "Sorry I brought it up." She pouts.

"Oh, baby, I know I can't wrestle forever. I'm already fat and old and all beat up."

"What you thought about doin' in your retirement?'

"I don't know. I thought about maybe buyin' a sheep ranch or somethin' in Utah."

"Sheep? Oh, yuck, Sammy!"

Tonight Candy has on a sequined body suit and piles her long hair up in a complicated way so that she looks like a country-western singer, and she and Samson go together to the Dallas Gardens, where she sits in the same front-row seat she had eleven months ago when Samson asked Gary The Giant to throw him out of the ring and at her feet so that he could introduce himself.

He had noticed her on four previous occasions. She always sat next to a curvy blonde girl he later found out was a friend of hers named Marilyn, who also worked at Sears, Roebuck. Marilyn was divorced. She had gotten married when she was fifteen to a boy named Jimmy Monroe mainly so that her name would be Marilyn Monroe. Candy and Marilyn cheered him—Bible Bob—on with their shrill country yells, jumping to their feet every few seconds, waving pretty little fists with pink-painted nails and twitching their shapely bottoms in such a way that the cowboys and rednecks and factory workers behind them whistled for *them*, the hell with the guys in the ring. Samson had had trouble keeping his mind on his job and got punched a couple of times because he was only half paying attention to what his opponent was doing. In his dimly lit, lonely Dallas motel room, green paint peeling off the walls and ceiling, he lay on the bed, picturing the dark-haired girl's white teeth and pink tongue, her breasts—squeezed his eyes shut and imagined dark purplish nipples. The blonde was also hot but reminded him too much of his first wife, Macy, so that when he tried to fantasize about her he'd end up thinking of Macy being screwed by Siamese twins.

When Gary The Giant threw Bible Bob out of the ring and at the girls' feet, Samson raised his head, smiled, and said, "Would either or both of you ladies like to have a late supper with me tonight?" Candy immediately said she would. Bible Bob leaped to his feet with a whoop, climbed back into the ring, and defeated Gary The Giant prematurely.

Sitting in an Italian restaurant lit only by the candles on the tables, Samson listened to Candy talk about her job as a sales girl at Sears, Roebuck and how she had never known how mean people could be until she got a job; about how she truly loved the excitement of professional wrestling, a sport she had only recently discovered; about her daddy she loved more than anybody or anything in the world; about her beautiful but nasty mama who tortured her poor daddy with stories of how her looks could have caught her a rich husband instead of a failure. Her white teeth glistened in the candlelight. "When Mama was fourteen, she had a boyfriend kill another man over her," Candy told him. "She still writes love letters to this man, Burt, that's in prison for life. She says to Daddy, `Now that's love. That's love when you'll kill another man over a girl. And I bet Burt would be makin' a lot of money if he wasn't locked up.' Daddy just drinks and tries to buy her nice things when he can. I've always tried to be a real good girl and be nice to Daddy to make up for him havin' such a miserable life."

"That's real sad," Samson said.

"You remind me of my daddy."

"Oh." Samson had a sinking feeling, stared at the flickering candle on their table. If it went out, he wouldn't be able to see her at all.

"But in a good way."

Samson told her he had been married once, twenty years ago to a phony blonde who swallowed swords and did tricks with lions and clowns.

The candle stayed lit; he slurped his spaghetti as quietly as he could; and she agreed to see him again.

Only after he'd taken her out for three months (to movies, fancy restaurants, nightclubs) and bought her hundreds of flowers and fifty or sixty pounds of expensive candy did she go to bed with him. And her hesitation gave him comfort, assured him she was no whore; that is, if she wasn't playing him for a fat old fool, trying to get out of him as many free meals and flowers as she could, while when he wasn't around she laid every cowboy in the city. For those three months, she'd kiss him, nice and wet, with some tongue action, but she kept her knees together. When she finally gave in (and he was always trying), she said it was because she loved him: he was a big sweet old thing—mature, funny, interesting, and wise. And she knew he loved her, too. He did—he sure did, he blubbered. He wept, his head buried between her comforting breasts, believing for the moment that they were the source of all the emotional and sexual nourishment he would ever need.

Before the bout, Bible Bob, as friendly and as happy as can be, explains to the weasel-faced little cologne-stinking television announcer that his mission in life is to kick butt for God.

"Tell us, Bible Bob, how will you fend off Igor Tolstoy, The Mad Russian's, nefarious paralyzer hold?"

With a big friendly smile Bible Bob, wearing a white wrestling suit with a white cape that helps hide his fat, looks straight into the camera: "All I can say is that Jesus is in my corner. I hope to get my soul-saver hold on this Communist and transmit and transfer to him some of the love I have. I love everybody 'cause I got Jesus in my heart. And Jesus is love."

"So, Bob, you never hate anyone?"

"Never. I love everybody, even the people that I have to kick their butts."

During the bout, as he and Igor grapple and punch and poke and kick, Samson can occasionally glance at his prize and the people around her: cowboys, fat slum women and their retarded-looking kids, angry frail men who work in warehouses and factories, winos dragged in off the streets because the TV people like a full arena. Candy screams for Bible Bob to mutilate that no good Russian, Igor Tolstoy, whose red wrestling suit bears on the front and back the Soviet hammer and sickle. People's faces are twisted, red, sweaty. They want Igor Tolstoy dead. Bible Bob can do all the loving as far as they're concerned—they hate that Communist bastard's guts. Bible Bob can do all the loving he wants as long as he also does some good butt kicking. The fans cheer him on. They seem to think it's real.

Samson loves being Bible Bob. He loves it as much as he ever loved being Samson The Strong Man, even during his time as world champion. When he becomes Bible Bob, he can forget all his problems—he doesn't think about Hoffman or anything else.

It is his destiny to win, to always win. He is Righteousness triumphing over Evil. Although Bible Bob often appears to be on the brink of defeat, he swells at the moment of crisis with the power of God, rises up, and vanquishes his opponent.

Toward the end of tonight's match, Igor has Bible Bob on the ropes, stamping his foot on the canvas to make a lot of noise as he throws a rapid succession of punches, and the fans are furious. A chant of "Kill the commie" starts up. Bible Bob groans and calls, "Lord, don't forsake me!"

An old woman fifteen rows from the ring stands and screeches, "Please, sweet Jesus, help the man!"

Samson raises his right arm, spreads his fingers, and jerks his head with each of Igor's punches, Igor's knuckles wheezing past his chin an inch away. It is strange how Samson's fingers tingle when he splays them and calls to God. It is spooky and wonderful. He needs to convince Hoffman to let Bible Bob become world champion.

Eventually, Bible Bob ducks away from the punches, picks Igor up, and does a back-breaker across his knee. Then while Igor—now a cowardly instead of a mad Russian—is on his knees, shaking his head and pleading with raised arms for mercy, Bible Bob places his right hand on Igor's forehead and shouts, "Out! Out all demons! Love! Love shall defeat you! Love!"

Igor faints, topples over backwards, and the fans get excited because they think he's maybe dead, but he remains unconscious only long enough to be counted out by the referee. Then crawling on his knees, he follows Bible Bob around the ring, Bob strutting and waving, Igor shouting in an accent that is a mixture of Mississippi redneck and TV Russian, "Oh, thank you! I seen the light, comrade!"

Samson loves this part, loves saving souls—wonders for a moment whether Ray felt this way when he was a preacher and saved people for real—but he always notes a certain disappointment in the applause.

The fact is, Samson knows, most of the fans would rather see Bible Bob's opponents dead than saved.

FOURTEEN

MR. CLEAVER IN PAJAMAS

After the wrestling match, Samson and Candy meet Marilyn Monroe for a late supper at an all-night diner downtown. Marilyn is going through another in a long series of crises. The three of them sit in a red vinyl booth, Marilyn across from Samson and his prize. Samson eats an entire baked chicken, along with mashed potatoes, corn, green beans, and biscuits. He drinks buttermilk. After he loosens his belt, he feels capable of having some cherry pie with vanilla ice-cream. Marilyn always depresses the hell out of him with her stories about the lousy men she gets involved with. Her boyfriends lie to her, take her money, beat her up, then vanish. She's only twenty, but she's been engaged nine times in addition to the one marriage. She gets engaged on first dates sometimes. Samson could tell her what's going on, what her problem is, but he doesn't know how to without his words coming out wrong and maybe hurting her feelings: men tell her they love her and want to marry her because they want to screw her; they're lying bastards, and she's stupid enough to believe them.

"This latest guy, Hank," Marilyn is saying, "seemed real nice. I let him borrow my car, and I buy him some real expensive pajamas—I like a man in pajamas, I don't know why. Like on `Leave It to Beaver' the other night, there's Mr. Cleaver in pajamas. I forget what the show was about, but there he is—Wally and Beaver's dad—in pajamas, and here I am never giving a second thought to Mr. Cleaver before, but when I see him in these pajamas, with a kind of classy little stripe in them, I'm thinking he's a real attractive man." She stops and sucks on the straw in her glass of Coke.

"What about Hank?" Candy asks.

"Huh?"

"You started to say something about Hank." Candy is eating just a wing from Samson's chicken. She's always saying she's afraid of getting fat.

"Oh, yeah, well..." Marilyn makes a face, twists it up so that she looks pretty ugly. "Turns out Hank—the man of my dreams, my prince in shining... or knight in whatever—is ...*married*!" Marilyn hangs her head, is maybe crying.

"Married?" Candy gasps.

Samson mumbles, "Son of a bitch."

"He's got kids and everything. His wife calls me up and says, `Is this Hank's fiancee?' I say, `Yes, it is. May I help you?' And she says, `This is Hank's wife.'"

"What did you say?" Candy's mouth hangs open, and she leans forward on the table.

"I say, `Maybe we're talkin' about two different Hanks.' And she says, `I'm talkin' about the Hank with the tattoo of a horse underneath his belly button.' Well, when she said that I just burst out in tears. She was nice about the whole thing, really. Not real friendly or anything, but I mean she wasn't blaming me. She didn't want to cut my throat or anything, and I guess I oughta be glad for that much. Turns out I'm not the first girl Hank's done this to."

Candy reaches across the table, takes Marilyn's hand, and says, "Oh, Marilyn, I'm so sorry."

"Yeah," Samson says.

Marilyn sniffles. "I gave myself to him. I gave him *everything*. You know what I mean?"

"Oh, hon, don't worry 'bout that," Candy says. "You oughta be past worryin' 'bout that with all your.... I mean, you know what *I* say—if a cat can have nine lives, then a girl's got the right to have nine virginities."

Samson gives Candy a sharp look. She pats his knee, and while Marilyn stares into her Cherry Coke, Candy shrugs and shakes her head at him to let him know she's just trying to cheer Marilyn up.

Marilyn dabs her eyes with a napkin and blubbers, "Well, I wish a cat had *sixteen* lives."

FIFTEEN

DICKS

In bed with Candy at two-twenty-five in the morning, Samson can't sleep. For one thing, his back hurts—more because of Candy's love than because of Igor Tolstoy's hate. She is softly snoring and drooling a little from the side of her mouth, which is half open. Her teeth are small, white—perfect. He watches her sleep, the way he watches Tina Lee sometimes, the way he used to watch Daryl Junior (who's almost all grown up now, a crazy teenager), the way he still watches Benny Bob and Earl.

Earl just turned eight, born that wonderful world championship year of 1954.

Samson pats Candy's head, and his heart swells. He feels tears well up. Does Hoffman know about her, too? If he knows about Darlene, he probably does.

But does he really know anything? If he does, how did he find out? Samson's been so careful.

Private eyes? Detectives? Dicks. Guys with little cameras and snub-nosed revolvers.

He eases out of bed and goes into the kitchen and sits down at the table, where his unfinished model of a '32 Packard is. He has been sloppy with it. Glue bubbles out of the seams. Threads of dripping glue have hardened on the fenders. There's a pile of pieces he hasn't figured out what to do with yet.

He gets up and takes the phone receiver off the wall and dials Hoffman's house. After a dozen rings, a woman answers. "Yeah? Who is this? Christ, what time... ? Hello?"

Samson pictures the platinum hair, the big tits floppy in some little nightgown. "Can I talk to Hoffman?"

She doesn't say anything. Then Hoffman is on the line. "Who is this?"

"It's Sam."

"Daryl? Where are you? You in trouble?"

"I gotta talk to you right now 'bout this Mexico business."

"Oh." His voice fades, and he says to his wife, "It's one of my wrestlers." Samson hears her laugh. "So, Daryl, you've been thinking about Mexico. That's good. I promise you it's going to be great. The Demon will be a big hit with all the fans down there bombed on tequila. They'll go home and have nightmares about you."

"I wanta know," Samson whispers, "more 'bout what you know."

"We'll work something out with the money. Maybe we can even cut a match or two from your circuit above the border so you won't have to be away from your loved ones so much."

"What do you know, Hoffman?" he hisses into the phone, his mouth on the receiver. His own hot breath blows back in his face.

"I'm not clear what you mean. I'm still a little groggy, Daryl."

"You know what I mean."

"I do?"

"Yeah."

"Hey, do you know what time it is?"

Then Samson hears Hoffman's wife say, "Tell the asshole to jerk off."

"Hoffman, tell me."

"Listen, I don't know what you want me to tell you, Daryl. I can give you more details about Mexico in a couple of days after the lawyers get back to me."

Samson's hand hurts from gripping the phone so hard. He takes a deep breath, relaxes. "Sweet, Jesus," he whispers happily.

"What, Daryl?"

"Nothin'. Nothin'."

It is like the moment thirty-five years ago when he realized he no longer believed in Martians that ate people's brains.

Relief.

Hoffman knows nothing. He's just a butterball going bald faster than Samson is.

Nothing.

"Listen, Hoffman, I'm sorry I woke you up, but what I got to tell you is I ain't wrestlin' no bouts in Mexico."

There is silence, then the tolling of the grandfather's clock in the living room. Three gongs.

"Listen, Daryl," Hoffman says sweetly, "I appreciate you wanting to let me know your decision right away. I'm sure you've been lying there in your motel room thinking all this over carefully, missing your family and thinking how you want to see them more instead of less. But Houston isn't so far from some of those border towns."

"Huh?"

"It is Houston where your family is, isn't it? It's not like they're way up in Oklahoma City or somewhere else."

Without another word, Samson hangs up the black phone.

SIXTEEN

THE DEMON

He turns out the kitchen light and sits in the dark, trembling, then gets up and paces. He can see all the love going out of his life—Darlene, Candy, Rachel Marie—all falling away from him into some black hole. Mama, too—she'll disown him, ashamed to call him her son.

And maybe he deserves it—whatever he gets. Hoffman isn't the only son of a bitch in the world. Or Marilyn's boyfriend Hank.

He thinks about spanking Tina Lee last night, spanking her because he hated himself. Now did that make any kind of goddamn sense? He is always telling Darlene to shut that child up or to clean that dirty child up or to make the kid eat her food so she won't grow up lacking brain cells and be a retarded person like he thinks her mother is sometimes.

God, he is a bastard. A monster.

God, little Tina Lee is the sweetest thing, all soft and round and pretty and pink, just like her mama, who is going to be a mama again.

He goes into the bedroom and crawls in next to Candy, his incredible prize. She's ten times better looking than John Kennedy's wife. Samson is luckier than the president of the United States.

Then suddenly, being in bed with Candy seems like something he has no right to; it makes him feel more and more like a son of a bitch who doesn't deserve to live and have three fine women and four beautiful children, to have so much love, so much love that his heart can barely hold it all.

He gets up and goes into the bathroom and sits on the toilet with the lid down. So much love. That is why he cannot give up any of his families: he loves them all, although loving them all is wrong and makes him sick in his soul.

How, *how*, with so much love can he be such a son of a bitch?

Because he wants to believe that there is some kind of order in the world, that chaos can fit together in a certain way so everything will make sense, Samson wonders if his being a son of a bitch, a bastard, and a monster has anything to do with being a bad guy wrestler most of the time these days. Maybe that's it. Hoffman, by making him become The Masked Demon, has ruined him. He hates being a bad guy, despite the fact he's pretty damn good at it (sometimes he even brags to Darlene about how he can really rile up the fans).

The Masked Demon—Hoffman's idea. Samson wears a red mask over his whole head with narrow slits for his eyes, nose, and mouth. And a red wrestling suit with long sleeves and pants legs, the whole thing so tight everybody can see every roll of fat and the bulge of his private parts—and a tail, a long pointed tail, which he sometimes wraps around his opponents' necks and sometimes trips over.

In the TV interviews he grabs the microphone from the announcer and yells, "I love evil, I love blood, I love death!" When the announcer tries to retrieve the microphone, The Demon shoves him so hard the announcer falls down on his butt. Then The Demon kicks him. The Demon says, "You want this back, wimp?

You want this back? Okay! Okay!" Then he wraps the cord around the man's throat and starts choking him.

While The Demon laughs sadistically, the announcer waves his arms, gasps for air. He looks into the TV camera and whines, "Please help me. Someone help... me. Oh, my goodness. Let's just go... to... ah... a commercial... bre—break. I'll be back... fans. I... hope...."

In the middle of a match, the hissing, booing spectators will shout to the deaf, dumb, and blind referee that The Masked Demon has just thrown in the eyes of Cowboy Chuck Carlson or Big Don Davis or Lucky Larry LaPue some red powder meant to burn a person's eyeballs right out of their sockets, and The Masked Demon will turn to the crowd and holler, "You better shut up! You better shut up!"

One night in Odessa a skinny man with a switchblade jumped into the ring and tried to cut The Demon's tail off and ended up tripping and stabbing himself in the thigh and then getting his arm broken by a security guard, a big freckle-faced man who smiled when he heard the skinny man's arm snap. Samson went to Hoffman afterward and said, "See what your ideas get."

Hoffman sat behind his desk, his electric fan blowing directly onto his fat face, and said, "Too bad it wasn't a televised match."

In Oklahoma City, an old white-haired man wearing a brown suit climbed into the ring and tried to knee The Demon in his private parts.

Recently there was the incident in Wichita Falls when a fat lady squeezed herself through the ropes around the ring and attacked The Demon with a hat pin.

For his first fifteen years as a professional wrestler, Samson was only one person: Samson The Strong Man, a good guy, a world champion in the southwestern United States of America. He loved that wide championship belt made of fake leather and gold-colored tin studded with red and blue and green pieces of glass. He loved it as if it had really meant something in the world of athletics, like an Olympic medal, and he supposes it did if people believed it did.

He was proud of himself because he knew he was good at what he did, even if it was just acting and acrobatics, and he always knew those first fifteen years who he would be from one match to another. But he'd gone flabby; his face puffed up and made his eyes beady; the fans got tired of Samson The Strong Man. After Stan Edwards died, Hoffman came onto the scene and told him that a change was overdue.

The last year and a half Samson The Strong Man has appeared only in Houston and is sometimes a bad guy. "How can I—he—be bad?" Samson asked Hoffman last year.

"It can happen. Look at what Samson in the Bible does. Whoring around. Drinking. Now am I wrong?"

"Samson The Strong Man" was the name he made up for his work in The Baldwin Circus and Carnival in 1936. Sitting in the bathroom of a house he shares with a woman he's not even married to, he remembers being young and righteous. Yes, righteous. He had prayed for the black, sin-damaged souls of clowns and trapeze artists and fire eaters and geeks and Siamese twins—just as his mama had taught him to always pray for people who were going to Hell but were foolish enough not to care. He prayed for his wife, Macy. Then he broke her nose. He prayed for the clown. Then he broke four of the clown's ribs. He prayed for himself.

The fear and heartache he feels now reminds him of what he felt then. He left the circus and got a job in a gas station in Iowa. He had decided to live simply, to stay to himself, to wait and see what God did with him. But his second day at the gas station, the owner, a fat man named Harold who slicked his black hair back with axle grease instructed him to let air out of people's tires while the gas was pumping so that they would think they needed to buy new ones. The owner grinned when he finished the instructions, showed his rotted teeth.

Samson needed the job, felt lucky he wasn't riding the rails like a lot of men in 1937. Harold was even letting him stay in a little room built onto the back of the gas station's garage. So he went along with the scheme for a week. He'd point out flat tires to people and say, "Looks like you got a... bad tire." The people often deflated the way their tires did. Their chests would collapse, their shoulders drooping forward. Their faces fell. If they didn't have the money, Harold would ask them what they had to trade.

For a week Samson could hardly sleep. He lost eight pounds. Then he started thinking that black bugs were swarming around him all the time. One night when he nodded off for a while, he dreamed of falling in a storm drain by the highway and being swept along by a flood. Leaves and dead birds swirled in the dirty water. And he was carried faster and faster along, deeper and deeper into the dark tunnel in the earth.

The next morning, near noon, a car pulled into the station, and Harold, who was replacing somebody's spark plugs with ones he'd taken out of a car a few days before, gave Samson a nod and mouthed, "Need to sell some tires, boy."

A thin, tired-looking lady and two little girls got out of the car. The lady said she'd like fifty-cents' worth of gas and asked Samson whether she and her daughters could use the rest room. He nodded. "It's round back, Ma'am."

Samson crouched down, stuck a little stick into the valve of one of the rear tires, and it hissed flat in nearly no time at all.

When Samson pointed it out to the lady, she said, "Oh, God. Oh, God, I don't know. A new tire?" The lady had light brown hair and wore a dress that had little flowers all over it. She laid her left hand on her cheek as if she had a tooth ache and Samson noticed her thin gold wedding band.

"Well, now, maybe... maybe... ," Samson stammered.

Harold came over, grinning his rotten grin and said, "Usually, you need to get at least two tires. They got to be matched. Ain't safe to have different tread types on a car, especially an old one like yours."

The two tall gas pumps with their round-glass heads stood above Samson, the lady, her kids, and Harold. The sun beat down. There was no breeze. Across the road was a field of Iowa corn stretching as far as Samson could see. A T-Model Ford puttered by on the road. And the lady started crying. Her little girls hugged her legs.

"Maybe you just need a patch job," Samson said.

The garage owner shot him a look.

"Only be seventy-five cents," Samson said.

"Now don't be hasty," Harold said. "Don't wanta just *patch* what might need *replacin'*." He looked at Samson. "You don't wanta send this lady and her little children off to their deaths on the highway just 'cause you think you can save 'em some money. I know you got good intentions, boy, but my God, money ain't everything." Harold turned to the lady. "Ain't that right, ma'am?"

"Well, it's just... just that I... don't... You sure it can't be patched?"

"Well," Harold said, "me and my assistant here can have a closer look once we get it off the rim, but I don't know. I wouldn't count on it, ma'am."

Samson couldn't look at the lady or her children or his boss. He stared across the road at the bright green and yellow corn field.

"If it's a matter of money, ma'am," the owner said, "I could maybe make you a deal. I mean, two tires are worth more than that skinny little gold ring you're wearin', but I might could do a trade."

Samson kept watching the corn field. Samson saw a breeze hit the corn stalks, sway them, before he felt it himself.

"My husband's dead," the lady said.

"Well, then don't matter much if you trade it for somethin' you really need."

Samson turned to the lady. "That's right. Harold here will give you two almost-new tires he took off a Chevrolet yesterday. Then he can sell the two tires he takes from you to somebody else this afternoon after I let air out of *their* tires."

The lady blinked several times, fast. "What? What do you mean?"

Harold stammered, "Oh... Boy's crazy. Don't—"

Her jaw dropped. "Am I being cheated?"

"No," Harold said with a big grin. "Course not. Boy's crazy, I tell ya. A circus freak. Don't know why I hired him."

"That's right. That's right, lady," Samson said. "I'm crazy. I'm a freak." He kicked over a stack of oil cans. He turned to Harold. "You lyin', cheatin' bastard." He stomped over to the air hose, pulled it to the lady's car and inflated her tire. "See. Nothin' wrong with that tire."

He and Harold watched the woman drive away. Then Harold looked at him. "You're fired, boy. You know that, right? You get out. You get out 'fore I take a notion to take a tire iron to ya."

Samson glared at him. He walked into the garage, picked up a tire, and ripped it in half with his bare hands.

Harold said, "Just go on now. I got a mind to call the sheriff."

Samson picked up another tire, ripped it in half. Then headed on down the road. Harold shouted after him, "You done cheated the people too. If you got a mind to tell the sheriff, you goin' down with me, boy!"

After he had walked a few miles, he lay down in a corn field and slept twenty hours—awoke on a bed of corn husks with rain pouring, soaking him through.

SEVENTEEN

VAMPIRE

No, he decides. No. The roles he plays as a professional wrestler are no excuse—that is all he is trying to do: make excuses. He is simply a bastard.

A son of a bitch.

A monster.

Candy opens the bathroom door and flicks on the light. Samson slaps his hands over his eyes, groans, feels for a moment as though he will burn up like a vampire exposed to sunlight. Finally, he peeks through his fingers. Candy stands in the doorway, kind of slouchy, her eyes half closed. She's naked. "Sammy?"

"What?"

"What you doin'?"

"Nothin'."

"Oh." She yawns. "Well, I gotta trickle."

"I need to be alone. Turn out the light."

"I gotta trickle."

"I wanta be alone, baby."

"I gotta trickle real bad."

"Not now, woman." His sudden anger is mixed with the thought that she's looking at him and noticing in this harsh light what a big fat blob he is.

"Sammy," she drones, "I gotta trickle like a water fall's gotta fall. You want me to trickle on your feet?"

He still has his eyes covered. He sighs. "Do you have to talk like some goddamn kid?" Young women are all children. Darlene with her door slamming and shouting and Candy with her little-girl talk. Rachel Marie is the only real woman he knows. Why wasn't he content with just her?

"What's wrong, you big ole thang?" Candy says as she steps toward him. She puts her slim arms around his head, one of her nipples right under his nose, and he starts to get hard. But when she lays the side of her face on top of his head in a loving way, he yells, "Ouch! Goddamn it! Watch my bruises."

"What?" She separates the strands of his graying, thinning hair to see bruises made by a bronze ashtray. "You got these tonight? You poor ole thang."

In his mind appears Darlene, scarlet-faced, mad as a hornet, wielding that bronze ashtray. He deserved it; he's sorry. But his ears and the back of his neck start burning with anger at Candy. "Quit, damn it!" He doesn't want her examining his bruises; he doesn't want her looking at his bald spot and gray hairs. He knocks her hands away.

"Honey, I just—"

"Get out!"

"I gotta trickle!"

He stands up, his belly jiggling, and stomps out. He stops outside the door, turns, and what he says just spews out like vomit; he can't help himself. "Whore bitch!"

"What you call me?" She's wide awake now.

"Whore bitch."

"You know I ain't."

"You ain't, huh? What's this about a girl havin' twenty-nine virginities? I never heard such shit. You didn't hang around them wrestlin' contests for nothin'. I'm gonna ask Jake The Snake 'bout you. He knows all the whores in Dallas. I can just see you with every wrestler... With every cowboy."

Stars are popping and flashing everywhere, as if someone were taking pictures. Private dicks.

"You're crazy."

"You... you and Kennedy. You and... and—"

She throws a big jar of face cream and it hits him square on the nose. He staggers back, and she slams the bathroom door and locks it. As bad as Darlene.

He fumes a few seconds, his nose throbbing, then kicks the door open. Splinters fly. The doorknob falls and rattles on the floor. Candy is backed against the bathtub, holding in front of her in one hand the safety razor she uses to shave her legs. Her breasts are heaving. Her black eyes are flashing. Her perfect teeth are bared. His foot hurts like hell.

Damn, she looks good, naked and flushed, all fired up, the tendons in her pretty neck bulging, the muscles in her thighs taut. He is about to melt. He wants to fall to his knees, crawl to her and beg for forgiveness—hug her legs and lick her pussy.

But she explodes with, "Who have *you* been screwin'?" And the razor rips the air.

Samson drives his fist into the wall. Plaster crumbles, dust billows out from the hole, gets into his nose. Jesus, his hand hurts. And his foot. His nose. He sneezes from the dust. Jesus, he just wants to be dead. *Come and save me, Lord.*

He hobbles into the bedroom, quickly pulls on some clothes, and for the second consecutive night, he is on the road.

EIGHTEEN

JAKE THE SNAKE'S DOGS

Jesus Christ. That's who Samson thinks he sees for a moment as he barrels down the highway at four-fifteen in the morning. His Cadillac's high beams catch a thin, bearded, hollow-eyed figure in baggy clothes holding up a hand, beckoning. But it's just a hitchhiker, a bum.

Even if he were in a better mood, Samson wouldn't stop for him. Stink up the car. Talk about how he once met some president or used to be a millionaire. Samson used to pick up hitchhikers, but he learned his lesson. They're almost always bums who will talk your ear off with crazy crap. Met President Roosevelt. Was good friends with Gary Cooper in high school, used to race hot rods and pick up girls together. Killed seventy Japs single-handed in one day on an island in the Pacific and escaped just before a volcano erupted and the island sank into the ocean—"Wish I still had my silver star to show ya." Screwed Doris Day in high school. Screwed Betty Gable in high school. Screwed Debbie Reynolds in college. Screwed Rosemary Clooney in the back of a Studebaker. Screwed the woman—"Lord, buddy, can't even remember her name now, oh well"—the woman who plays Ma Kettle in the movies: "Well, buddy, I mean, she needed love, too, just like everybody else."

One old bum claimed that he was Ty Cobb, the baseball player, and that he had a million dollars in the paper bag he held on his lap; he also said he had a loaded German Luger in the bag and wasn't afraid to use it if some bastard got ideas about his money. He was the craziest old coot of them all. When Samson let him out of the car, Ty reached into the bag, took out a two-dollar bill, autographed it, handed it to him, and said, "You know, Hitler wasn't so bad."

Samson barrels along at eighty, ninety, ninety-five. When he left Candy's house, he headed out of Dallas in the direction of Donie with the idea of going to his mama's house, but after a few miles, he saw a sign for the road to Potosi, and now he's on it. He's not sure yet of exactly what he's going to do, but making this morning a day of vengeance seems like a good idea. Vengeance overdue.

Jake The Snake lives in Potosi.

Samson drives faster, faster. He has to beat the dawn. He fiddles with the radio but decides all he wants is the whistle of the wind and the rush of the air conditioner turned on high. At a hundred and ten miles an hour, he flies through the black world outside his windows.

He glances over at the passenger seat and sees in the dim green glow of the dash lights the new issue of *Goliath* magazine. Iron Man Mike is on the cover, a cocky red-headed kid in his mid-twenties whose head is way too small for his muscle-bound body. He looks like a freak Samson knew in The Baldwin Carnival and Circus. Iron Man Mike wears a cocky grin and the world championship belt. Samson opens his window and tosses the magazine out.

Samson has been on the cover of *Goliath*—four times in fact—but not since 1955. Seven years ago. He thinks about that.

He picked up the latest issue at the arena last evening and carefully looked through it before his bout with Igor Tolstoy, searching for any mention of Samson The Strong Man, Bible Bob, or The Masked Demon. In the cover story about Iron

Man Mike, Mike promised to unmask The Masked Demon. Speculation is that The Demon is an escaped murderer or a well-known politician. There was no mention anywhere in the magazine of Samson The Strong Man or Bible Bob.

This latest issue had yet another story about Bobby Shine. An anonymous source contacted the editors of *Goliath* with the amazing story that Bobby Shine faked his death in 1954 so that he could become a secret agent for the United States government and help defend the country against the Communist threat. "The White House, the FBI, and the CIA all refused to respond to the inquiries posed by the editors of *Goliath*, thereby raising suspicions that the anonymous caller's allegations possessed more than a little validity."

Samson, watching the needle of the speedometer flirt with a hundred and twenty and thinking about the Bobby Shine story, gets even madder than he already was. Shine is dead. Dead. Rotted in the ground. "I work my butt off," Samson says aloud. "A cocky kid and a dead man get more attention." He slaps the dashboard. Shit, his hand hurts. And his foot. His nose. Also, the top of his ear, the one mutilated by Jake The Snake. The part that hurts is the part that's gone. Phantom ear.

Samson knows that Jake had a match in Altus, Oklahoma, last night. Today, he'll be in Lawton for a bout with Ed Powers, the former lineman for the Chicago Bears. Jake's house will be empty. Samson will probably be able to do whatever he wants to the place.

Jake used to be married, but his wife got smart years ago and walked out. Jake never mentions her, but he's always standing around in locker rooms before bouts, stinking up the place with his cigar and talking about some whore and every little disgusting thing she did to him. Or he talks about his dogs.

He has two hound dogs, a male and a female, to keep him company. He brags about what good hunting dogs they are, what good watch dogs they are, how they can do all kinds of incredible tricks (turn somersaults, count to seven). He claims they like to drink beer (they prefer Lone Star over all other brands); he wishes he could teach them to play poker, he has told Samson, and if he could get the one that's a bitch to give him blow jobs, he'd be content to avoid all contact with human beings.

Samson decides he'll kill them. He'll take the jack handle out of his Cadillac's trunk and smash their dog brains all over Jake The Snake's house.

He touches his ear. From the start way back in 1945, Samson The Strong Man's opponents have often tried to cut his hair. He got scratched and stuck slightly with a lot of scissors over the years before the night Jake The Snake decided a pair of shrub shears would be more dramatic than scissors, like a big gun as opposed to a little gun. Baby Bruce—who was sometimes Jake The Snake's partner in tag-team bouts and whose gimmick was that he sucked giant lollipops before matches and wailed like a baby whenever an opponent hurt him—stood by the ring and handed the big black-handled clippers to Jake, the blades gleaming like jewels, while Samson The Strong Man lay unconscious from Jake's sleeper hold.

Jake has claimed that the accident was actually Samson's fault because he started to regain consciousness a moment too soon and turned his head just as Jake was going to snip a little lock of his hair off. It was going to be just two or three inches that Jake would hold up proudly and show off to the TV announcer after the match.

There was the grating and squeaking of the blades sliding against each other, the awful sound piercing his eardrum, and then the sudden, shocking, sharp, burning pain. Samson jumped up screaming, clutching the side of his head. His hand came away red. Blood ran down his face, his neck, his shoulder, his arm. At the sight of that sad little hunk of meat, a half circle, lying on the canvas, he fainted.

Samson has never been to Jake The Snake's house, but he knows Potosi is not a big place. On the outskirts of town, he sees a phone booth at a gas station, pulls up next to it, and gets out. Inside the lit-up gas station, a sleepy-looking attendant sits sprawled on a wooden chair and watches Samson. He thinks about asking the attendant for directions, but decides he'd better not. He turns his back to the guy and looks up "Jackson Lee Hinterlong" (Jake's real name) in the phone book to get the address. When he turns around, the attendant is standing behind him, a tall long-faced man with buck teeth. On his shirt pocket is the name Waldo. It's one of Samson's real names, one he hasn't mentioned to anyone since he was about seven years old.

"Can I help ya, mister? Ya need some gas?"

"No. No." Samson avoids making eye contact. "Just passing through. Not stopping nowhere. Got plenty of gas."

"Fine lookin' Caddy."

Samson nods, ducks into his Cadillac and drives away—probably too fast. He's shaky for a minute, but then decides he's here and he's still going to Jake's house. The hell with Waldo. The hell with everybody.

By the time Samson finds the street, the sky is beginning to lighten. Jake's house is at the end of a dead-end dirt lane. Railroad tracks run a couple of hundred feet behind it. Samson parks in the road, keeps the engine running. He looks around. The windows of the neighbors' houses are dark.

Jake's house is constructed from white-washed concrete blocks and has a flat tin roof. Three rusty old cars—a Hudson, a Plymouth, and a Buick—sit in the front yard. The driveway is empty. The grass is dead. The neighbors' places look pretty much like Jake's. Samson thinks about what Jake spends money on: a new Lincoln Continental each year and expensive suits and expensive cigars and a lot of booze and five or six whores a week. The fool.

Samson opens his Cadillac's trunk and takes out the jack handle. It feels heavy. He's sweating now, and his heart is thumping. Goddamn dogs. Goddamn Jake. Goddamn Hoffman. Goddamn women who never appreciate all you do for them—save them from having to work, save them from men who would be mean to them. Darlene and Candy could have ended up like that girl Marilyn.

Son of bitch, his gut suddenly hurts, and he thinks he might puke. His chest hurts, too. Heart attack, he thinks. Like his daddy. "Please, God, let me kill the dogs first."

His heart burns with hate, with envy, with frustration. Bible Bob should be world champ, not Iron Man Mike.

He has a vision—a sharp-focused remembrance of the fat lady with the hat pin coming at him, The Masked Demon. He hates being hated. Maybe he should start wearing a bullet-proof vest under the red wrestling suit.

The backyard is full of dog turds. Two dog houses stand in the middle of the yard. They're big clapboard constructions painted white—painted recently it looks like—with green trim around the doors and around the little windows on the sides. The roofs are peaked and have green shingles. Above the doors there's fancy gingerbread trim on which the dogs' names are painted in red: "Mona" and "Ralph." Samson remembers Jake saying he named his dogs after an old girlfriend and his brother.

The chain-link fence around the yard is about four feet high. The dogs are asleep inside their houses, their rear ends sticking out the doors.

He will wake them up. He will stay outside the fence. When they run over to him, barking and snarling and foaming at the mouth, he will raise the jack handle over his head and then bring it down with every ounce of strength in his body. Crunch. A few more hits. Splat. Simple enough.

Samson looks around at the house next door. A black joy fills his chest.

Then the ground is shaking. At first, he doesn't know what's happening—Oh, lord!—then realizes a train is coming. The train's roar builds as he glares at the dogs' rear ends and slaps his left palm with the jack handle. The roar builds until his whole body vibrates with it. His false teeth rattle.

The train rattles and whistles.

Finally, the roar fades, and he whispers, "Here, doggy, doggy. Here, Mona. Here, Ralph."

The dogs stir. He expected them to race at him, leap onto the fence, fangs wet, hot dog breath like fire in his face. But they heave themselves up slowly, crawl backwards out of their houses, and amble over to him. A couple of old hound dogs with sad, droopy jowls.

Except for the husky breathing of the dogs, the morning is silent now. The sun spies on Samson from the edge of the earth. The sky pales above his head, is a dozen colors on the horizon. He stares at the dogs' big watery eyes. He cannot believe that these humble, decrepit, gentle things are connected with Jake The Snake. Samson stares at the fancy dog houses. Then he looks at Jake's house and imagines Jake lying in bed at night listening to rain on the tin roof.

Jake loves these animals. Truly loves them. And they probably love him.

Samson hears the squeak of a screen door and turns toward the next-door neighbor's house. A wiry man in boxer shorts and cowboy boots stands on the stoop of his back door, squinting at Samson. "Hey. Hey, you. What you doin'?"

Samson drops the jack handle and bolts. His foot hurts. His knees hurt. His chest aches. His head fills with a roar. Another train. But when he looks back he doesn't see one.

To his horror, the Cadillac has stalled. He turns the key, pumps the gas pedal. He looks over his shoulder and sees the wiry man coming after him with the jack handle. The engine turns over but doesn't catch. It grinds and grinds.

"Hey, you. Hey, fat boy! Stop, you long-haired son of a bitch!"

The engine finally catches, and the Cadillac's tires dig into the dirt. The car shimmies, then shoots forward.

Samson's chest hurts like hell. His stomach churns. His foot hurts. His hand hurts. His nose hurts. His ear hurts. Oh, he deserves to hurt. He is a son of a bitch. God is punishing him for being evil.

Samson has sense enough to watch his speed. He wonders whether the police will check the jack handle for fingerprints. He doesn't know why he dropped it. Stupid.

The wiry man probably read his license plate. Lord.

But a few miles down the road, with no sirens approaching, he tells himself he did nothing. Only if someone could read his mind would anyone know that he was guilty of attempted premeditated dog murder. But he didn't even attempt. He just thought about it, got prepared to do it. Then did nothing.

Still, he is a bastard. Jesus, what a son of a bitch. A monster. Sweet Darlene. Sweet Tina Lee. He wonders how Darlene is getting along. Her mama will have to come and stay when it's time for the baby to arrive.

Candy. He's never had a bad fight with her before. He sees a gas station up ahead and skids across its gravel lot up to the building.

Samson jumps out. "I got to use your phone. You got a pay phone?" he says desperately to a boy in a greasy pale-blue shirt, "Hiram" stitched across the pocket in fancy letters.

"Inside, mister. Somethin' wrong?"

Samson fumbles with nickels and dimes and quarters, the phone receiver cradled between his neck and shoulder. Candy's phone rings only once. "Baby, it's me. I'm sorry, baby. I love you. I'm just the biggest son of a bitch on earth..." Candy's crying. "You been cryin' all this time?"

"No. I'm... I'm not cryin' 'bout... that. I'm cryin' 'cause... 'cause I just found out somethin' awful."

"What is it, baby?"

"Marilyn Monroe ...."

"What?"

"She ...died. *Died*."

"Jesus, baby."

"It looks like she killed herself."

"Jesus. You think 'cause of that guy with the wife?

"What guy?"

"Jesus. I'll cancel my bouts and come right back there and go to the funeral with you. When's it goin' be?"

Candy sniffs. "Oh. I don't know. I can't go to the funeral."

"You can't? There some Catholic rule against goin' to other folks' funerals if they ain't Catholic?"

"It'll be in Hollywood or somewhere."

"Hollywood?"

NINETEEN

MAMA

In a couple of hours, the temperature is already ninety, the sun blazing down on Texas. In Donie, Samson stops at a gas station two blocks from his mama's house. Painted across the top of the building is "BODY WORK OIL CHANGE TUNE UP ALIGNMENT RADIATOR—THE BEST PLACE IN TOWN TO TAKE A LEAK!" He goes into the men's room (which is so filthy he holds his breath the whole time he's in there), and puts on a tie for his mama. His wearing a tie makes her proud. One of the things that upset her when Ray stopped being a preacher was that he no longer dressed nicely. Samson's tie is yellow with a green and red coconut tree on it.

He wets his comb and slicks down his long hair. He feels as though his lungs are going to burst.

He comes out of the men's room, gasping for air. The heat of the sun hits him, and he feels light-headed, sees spots, as he stumbles over to a pay phone at the corner of the garage. He dials Darlene's number, and it rings a dozen times before she answers. He says, "Honey, it's me. You okay?"

"I was just in the john, throwin' up my Corn Flakes. It's only normal, and besides, why should you care? You broke the damn screen door, you know that?"

"I'm sorry 'bout that. I was a crazy bastard."

"You need to see a head shrinker."

"I just been under a lot of pressure."

"What happened at that meetin' with Hoffman. You goin' be in a movie?"

Samson clears his throat. His chest hurts. "What? Oh, yeah. Yeah, he's got plans for me, but these things take a lot of time. I don't know what's gonna happen."

Darlene grunts. "Well, you think about seein' a shrinker 'cause I ain't puttin' up with much more of your madman shit. I'll divorce you."

"You say that at least once every week, hon. You know I need you."

"Tina Lee's cryin'. I gotta go."

"I love you, hon."

Darlene snorts like a hog and hangs up on him.

He calls a florist in Oklahoma City to have red roses delivered to Darlene. After he hangs up, he stares at the phone for a minute, then calls a florist in Dallas.

At his mama's house, he sits at the kitchen table. In front of him are five fried eggs and eight pancakes and a dozen buttermilk biscuits. Jars of jellies, sticks of butter, a glass of buttermilk, a cup of coffee. At one end of the old oak table there are gray stains where his daddy's sweat soaked into the wood. Daddy sweat a lot when he ate. It's hard to believe he's been dead twenty-two years.

"Eat," Mama says.

"I ain't hungry." He whispers because his sister is asleep. It's ten-thirty in the morning, but she has no reason to get up. Or she's just pretending to be asleep so that she won't have to see him. Poor Jean Anne, his twin sister, is a spinster, too huge for any man to handle. She weighs more than Samson does. One advantage Catholics have is that ugly girls can become nuns instead of just sad old maids.

"You eat now," Mama says, standing at the sink with her back to him, scrubbing the heavy skillet she's been cooking in ever since Samson can remember. She looks over her shoulder at him. "You look pale."

"What's Jean Anne doin' these days?"

"Same," says Mama, who is a tiny woman, not quite five feet. Deep liverish gouges underscore her eyes, and her wattled throat is a wreck of flesh. Her body is sinewy. "Same" means Jean Anne does nothing but help Mama clean house, eat enough for six women, watch "To Tell the Truth," "Queen for a Day," "General Hospital," "Days of Our Lives," and other game shows and soap operas. She reads nine or ten paperback science-fiction books a week.

"I wish Jean Anne didn't hate me," Samson says.

"Why, nobody hates you, Daryl Lee. Don't talk crazy. Now eat."

"She does hate me, and you know it. Ray does, too. It's because they think you think I'm some big success and they're nothin'. But they're really better than me. Jean Anne's here to help you. She's here if you ever need anybody. And Ray... Ray's a good bowler. He just needs some luck."

"Ray should of stayed a preacher is what *I* think," Mama says. Ray lives here with Mama also, when he's not on tour. This morning he's already at the bowling alley, Donie Bowl-O-Rama. Mama makes a sour face and goes on: "Bowls a bit and drinks like a fish. I used to be so proud of him." She shakes her head. She dries her hands and sits down across from Samson. "Now I'm gonna set here and watch you eat that food till it's all gone."

He starts eating, slowly at first. He eats and he thinks. His mama studies him lovingly.

"Them boys you wrestle been beatin' up on you good, it looks like. You want some salve?"

"Mama, I'm just a fake. I ain't nothin'. I ain't no more than some clown." He pauses and stares at her. "Listen, Mama, I been bad. I been bad a long time, and I'm gettin' worser."

His decision to confess all his sins to Mama is reckless, he knows, but he hopes she will have some special wisdom that sixty-six years on earth have given her, some advice that will save him. And he hopes she will have enough compassion and love to forgive him. After all, he's her boy. She nursed him on her titties till he was three years old. She used to remind him of that whenever he was bad. Even when he was a teenager and he'd get caught smoking or let a curse word slip, Mama would make him hold out his hands, palms up, to be whacked with a ruler, and she'd say, "To think I let you suck my titties till you was three." Samson would hang his head, his palms burning, and feel sick to his stomach.

Now, here he is, an old man of forty-three, and his mama reaches across the table, saying, "Those mean boys," across the food she fixed, to touch his nose and the bruises on his forehead, inflicting pain with each touch.

The smell of her powder and perfume float to him. In recent years she has become vain about her appearance and sits across from him now in a dark blue dress with white lace, a church dress. Whenever he shows up unexpected, like today, he has to wait in the living room while she runs to her bedroom and puts on a Sunday dress and her silver wig and smears rouge on her cheeks. Only then will she come and hug and kiss him, as if otherwise she is not worthy of receiving her guest, her own boy. Then she starts cooking—whether he wants her to or not.

"Mama, I know you're proud of me, but you shouldn't be. I'm not near as good a person as Jean Anne or Ray even."

"You're the one out there in that big old wild world makin' money and bein' famous. Ray ain't never been on TV with his bowlin'. Jean Anne won't never be on TV neither less she takes it in her mind some day to hit me over the head with a axe, which wouldn't surprise me she's so down in the mouth all the time."

"See. That's what I mean. It's you thinkin' of them that way makes them hate me. Jean Anne don't hardly ever come out of her room when I'm here."

"I love Jean Anne. You know that. She knows that. She does do a bit of sweepin' and washin' round here, but she don't live in no big brick house in Houston, and she don't have no fine family. I'm not odd, if that's what you think. I see Gladis Peters and them at church or at the Piggly Wiggly when I'm grocery shoppin', and they don't ask much 'bout Ray or Jean Anne, but they always ask 'bout you and your family."

"Oh, Mama." Samson wishes she wouldn't talk so loud. He cringes and looks over his shoulder at the doorway to see if Jean Anne is there or coming down the hall.

"You're a gifted athlete, Daryl Lee."

Samson sighs. "It's all fake, Mama. I been tellin' you for years. I'm a fake."

"I don't think so, Daryl Lee Douglas Ambrose Waldo Bierce. You know, I gave you a bunch of names 'cause I knew the day you and Jean Anne were born that you'd be somebody important."

"Why didn't you give a bunch of names to Jean Anne?"

"She was a girl, and you had a sparkle in your eyes and the fattest little wiener the doctor said he'd ever seen."

"Please, Mama... ."

"And I was right. Look at you now. Gifted athlete."

"It's fake, Mama."

"Don't look fake to me." She touches each of his bruises again.

"That hurts."

"See."

TWENTY

DADDY'S SWEAT

The phone rings, and Mama jumps up to get it. Samson hears her in the living room. "Well, hi, darlin'. You doin' all right? Ah, huh. How 'bout the boys? Yeah? You sure everything's all right, darlin'. Okay, okay. Well, this must be your lucky day 'cause my boy's right here. Let me get him for you." Mama shouts, "Daryl Lee, it's Rachel Marie!" Samson heaves himself up from the table and goes into the living room. "She thought you might stop by here," Mama says as she hands him the phone.

"Hello."

"Daryl," Rachel Marie says. "I was hoping you would stop by there. You need to get home tonight if you can. We've got trouble." Her voice is thin, brittle, like her body.

"What's wrong?"

"We just have to talk when you get here. I just wanted to make sure you came home tonight if you could."

"I'll be there tonight. I'm just vistin' with Mama right now. I was gonna stop by the bowlin' alley and see Ray, but I can skip that."

"No, it's not anything really urgent. I just hoped you'd come home tonight. You go ahead and stop and see Ray."

"One of the boys sick?"

"No."

"*You* sick?"

"No."

"Daryl Junior's in trouble again, ain't he?"

"We'll talk when you get home. It's just... ." Her voice breaks. She starts crying.

"Oh, honey—"

She gulps air. "Really... it's not anything we can't... can't deal with."

"Then why you cryin'?"

"I just wanted you to come home tonight. You visit with your mama and stop and see Ray. I'll see you tonight."

After he hangs up, Mama asks, "What Rachel Marie want? Everything all right?"

He shrugs. "She says we got trouble, but she wouldn't say what. I got to get home tonight."

"Well, if she didn't say on the phone, then it can't be anything real bad. Daryl Junior maybe got a bad grade on his report card or some little thing. Rachel Marie always makes a fuss over every bitsy thing."

Samson returns to the kitchen and finishes his breakfast, his heart full of worry. He eats and worries and wonders how his life got so complicated, like an eight-man, tag-team, death-cage, no-time-limit match. He's not smart enough to handle a complicated life.

He looks around the room. His life used to be simple. He wishes he could move in here with Mama and Jean Anne and Ray and watch TV all day and eat Mama's good cooking—stop worrying about women, about money, about wrestling, about kids, about his weight.

The little house has not changed much in over thirty years, except for the round-screen Motorola TV in the living room he bought in 1954 and the modern stove and refrigerator he bought a couple of years later, back when the money was pouring in and he had only one woman to support.

He stares at his daddy's sweat stains at the head of the table. Nobody ever sits in Daddy's place. At this very table, Samson arm wrestled him almost every evening, starting at the age of four, his daddy using one finger to beat him. Samson clearly recalls sitting on the wooden floor of the hardware store and watching Daddy carry two one-hundred-pound sacks of feed at once, one under each arm, out to a farmer's pick-up truck. Samson could do the same by the time he was thirteen. When he was fourteen, he beat his daddy at arm wrestling one evening. He jumped up from the kitchen table, whooping and hollering. He laughed at his daddy, who sat looking grim. That night he dreamed his daddy was dead, laid out on the kitchen table, and the undertaker came to the house and put silver dollars on Daddy's eyes and then shook Samson's hand and said, "Congratulations." Samson woke up, trembling and crying. He couldn't go back to sleep. In the morning, he asked Daddy to arm wrestle him before breakfast, and Daddy said, "Why? So you can laugh in my face again?" But Daddy sat down and put his elbow on the table. Samson let the contest last awhile, staring at Daddy's face, watched a bead of sweat slide down his temple, then let him win.

Daddy died at forty-seven. Samson is almost there. He wonders whether something in his genes is ticking like a time bomb. His chest hurts, worrying about it. Then again, death would be a way out of everything.

Suddenly, sitting in this kitchen that has never been free of the smell of biscuits in Samson's lifetime, he wonders whether his daddy ever cheated on Mama.

It is a stupid thought, he quickly decides. Daddy worked in the hardware store fourteen hours a day and loved Mama with the devotion of a true Christian man. The whole family went to church every Sunday and Wednesday. Daddy was a deacon.

Reverend Fuller sometimes pointed at men and women in the congregation and confronted them right there in front of not just God but their friends and neighbors about some rumor to the effect they had been drinking or wearing tight skirts or taking the Lord's name in vain or committing adultery. People were humiliated; they broke down and cried, begged for forgiveness—or they got mad and told the preacher he had no right and bolted from the church never to return. "Go on!" Fuller would shout. "Run, sinner! The devil is at your heels!" Some of the people moved out of town. Some people who were afraid of becoming future victims went elsewhere to worship, scared they would be pointed at and accused. The Methodist church and even the Baptist church were safer. But Daddy and the rest of the family never missed a service, and Daddy never once got pointed at.

Samson remembers the hard pews and sitting for hours in the hot little church in the middle of summer. The preacher wouldn't let people fan themselves. He had a sign on the altar that said, "NO FANNING." He wanted them all to swelter, to get a taste of Hell.

Reverend Fuller's face shone with sweat. When he flung his arms out in a grand gesture and shouted of eternal damnation, his sweat—Church of Christ holy water—sprayed out across the first few rows of the congregation.

His pinch-faced wife and scrawny, pale daughter sat in the front pew. The ladies in the church couldn't stand the uppity wife. The poor skinny daughter didn't have any friends either. Kids (Daryl Lee, too, a couple of times) used to throw pebbles and clods of dirt at her on the school playground for no reason except that she was shy and frail and got the top marks in every subject and that throwing things at her was kind of like throwing things at her daddy and, if you thought about it, kind of like throwing things at God—neither one of them wanted anyone to have any fun.

Funny how things turned out. Fate. Destiny. God doing His job. That frail girl, Samson's Rachel Marie.

TWENTY-ONE

THE DEVIL

Mama apologizes three times for the furniture being dusty as she buzzes around with a rag and can of spray wax.

"I ain't President Kennedy," Samson says.

Mama mumbles something about Catholics and keeps dusting. When he has eaten all the food she fixed, she clears the table. While she stands at the sink, washing the dishes, Samson feels guilty for never buying her a dishwasher. It's not right that Candy has one, but his own mama doesn't. Rachel Marie needs one, too.

Mama hums at the sink, happy to have her favorite child visiting.

"I wish Rachel Marie wasn't so mysterious on the phone," Samson says.

"How's the boys been gettin' along? Daryl Junior ain't wrecked no more cars, has he?"

"They're fine boys. Daryl Junior's almost a man and be calmin' down soon."

Samson hopes.

"Sure he will," Mama says. "I already got all their Christmas presents."

"Christmas ain't for five months, Mama."

"Jean Anne knows where they are if I pass away before then."

"Oh, Mama."

"You never know when the Lord's gonna come for you."

"You be around another forty years, Mama. Now don't make me sad. I'm sad enough."

"What you got to be sad about? You're just all wore out and beat up. They got you workin' too hard. Has Rachel Marie been feedin' you good? Her mama couldn't cook worth a lick. You remember those pot-luck suppers at the church? Everybody stayed a mile away from anything Mrs. Fuller cooked."

"Rachel Marie cooks fine. She's a good wife." He studies his big paws, which he has on the table. Big cuticles, big knuckles. His right hand is skinned up and bruised from punching Candy's wall. The back of each hand is furry. Wolf man. He is a monster, no denying it. "I don't deserve Rachel Marie. She's a brittle little woman. I worry 'bout her."

"You're a good husband, Daryl Lee. You're a good provider. A celebrity and all."

"Oh, Mama, you don't know how bad I am."

"You've been bad?" a voice behind him says. "Mama will never believe it." Samson shivers, is startled. Jean Anne has sneaked up on him, is standing in the doorway, blocking out any light coming from the hall.

"Well, hey, sister."

She waddles across the kitchen floor. She's wearing a robe that was green years ago and has faded to gray. Samson gets up so he can hug her, but she gives him a nasty look and says, "Don't get up. I just came in for my blood pressure pills. Ya'll go on with whatever you were doing." Her hair hangs to her shoulders, about the same length as Samson's, thin, oily, and the color of squash.

"How is your blood pressure?" he asks.

"The same."

"I could work you up a exercise program to help you lose weight."

"Sit down, Jean Anne," Mama says.

She ignores Mama and glares at Samson's belly and smirks. "Heard you've become The Devil," she says. "Why didn't you ever tell us?"

Samson is startled again—a man can't keep anything a secret. "Oh, it's just a new gimmick. The head promoter thought it up. I don't like it none. You know how stupid all that stuff is. I was just tellin' Mama 'bout how fake it all is."

"What's this about The Devil?" Mama asks.

"It ain't nothin' interestin', Mama."

Jean Anne says, "Come on, Daryl, tell us about it. Tell us about you being The Devil."

"Well, it ain't The Devil, Jean Anne. It's The Masked Demon. I'm called The Masked Demon in a couple of cities now. I wear—"

"I seen him on the television," Mama says. "Why aren't you on the television as much as you used to be? I haven't seen you in a month of Sundays."

Samson clears his throat and looks at his sister. "How you find out, Jean Anne?"

"Boyd Gleason at the Piggly Wiggly—he's the manager there now—said he was in San Antonio for a state convention of the Bison Lodge and went to the wrestling matches and thought that was you but wasn't sure. He said you were really good, if it was you." She pops a couple of pills into her mouth and takes a drink of water from a Fred Flintstone glass, the kind of glass a lot of gas stations are giving away; Samson has several in the backseat of his Cadillac to give to his younger boys, Earl and Benny Bob.

"He don't look like you," Mama says.

"What?"

"That demon man."

"It's just a act. I wear a mask."

"You're pullin' my leg."

Jean Anne sighs. "For Christ's sake, Mama, he's sitting right there admitting to you he's The Devil."

"The Masked Demon."

Mama says, "I don't believe it."

"It ain't important," Samson says. "Hey, Jean Anne, you sure are lookin' good. I mean, we could both stand to lose a few pounds, but I mean you look fine. Those pills help keep your blood regular, huh?"

Jean Anne has her back to him, pouring the leftover water from her glass into the sink. "I've got some things to do. Nice seeing you, Demon."

"Now don't run off. I'm gonna go see Ray. You wanta come? Bowlin' is good exercise."

"Too busy."

"Oh, come on. I don't hardly ever see you."

She flips up a hand on her way out of the room to say good-bye or go to Hell, probably both. Her old slippers shuffle; the sides of them are split. She was silent coming in, but she's noisy enough going out, scuffing up Mama's oak floor. Samson tells himself he has to buy her a new pair of slippers and bring them next time he visits.

When he and Jean Anne were little, they played together all the time (war usually—Mars vs. Earth), slept in the same bed, walked around town holding hands. Sometimes Mama would dress them both up as girls until Daryl Lee was as old as five or six. They shared their ideas about Mama and Daddy and God. They agreed that God was nice as long as you didn't get out of line—a giant with a white beard who could help you find a nickel on the ground or put Daddy in a generous mood when you were dying for a piece of candy or a Dr Pepper and who could reach down through the clouds and smack you around if need be.

They never played with Ray. Ray was a stiff little kid, five years older than they were but no bigger because he inherited Mama's tiny bones. He went to school in a black suit and carried a Bible and screamed in his squeaky voice at his classmates every day on the playground: "Ya'll *all* gonna *burn* in Hell! Tossed like twigs into the *fire!* Repent I say!" The kids would jeer at him for a while as he continued to rail at them. Then they would get bored with the whole situation and beat the crap out of him. He'd limp home, his suit tattered, his face bruised, and say to Mama, "God will strike them down."

When Daryl Lee and Jean Anne started school, they were the biggest kids in the first five grades. First grade was when life started turning sour for Jean Anne. It was fine for Daryl Lee to be kind of dumb at school work and big; it was awful for Jean Anne to be smart and big. Kids were cruel to her for no good reason. Ray kind of asked for what he got, Daryl Lee figured, but poor Jean Anne didn't bother anybody. She couldn't help it if she was smart, and she couldn't help it that she weighed a hundred and thirty pounds when she was seven years old. Daryl Lee beat up boys who called her names. She used to kiss his cheek and tell him he was the only child in their school, maybe on the whole planet, she did not hate. But as they got older, she started to resent him playing protector and said nasty things to him: "I don't need you beating up people for me. I'll do it myself. I don't need your help, dummy. I'll set a whole platoon of brain-eating Martians on you."

Occasionally, Samson recalls with great embarrassment how his fear of Martians all came back on Halloween night in 1938 when Orson Wells did *War of the Worlds*. He was back home after quitting the carnival and everything else, working in Daddy's store; Halloween night he walked into the living room, and an hysterical voice was coming out of the brand new Zenith radio Daddy had bought Mama for her birthday. The radio announcer was hollering that Martians had invaded Earth. Samson looked at Jean Anne, who was calmly sitting in the rocking chair nearby and reading a book. He said, "Lord, sister, you hear that?"

She looked up from her book and said, "You missed the first part."

The hysterical voice kept coming out of the radio, describing mass destruction throughout New Jersey. The reporter said the Army had been called out, but the Martians had superior weapons.

"The first part?" Samson asked. He felt light headed and had broken out into a sweat.

"Yeah. That reporter said eyewitnesses have seen these Martians wrestle people to the ground and suck their brains out through their ears."

Samson's mouth dropped open.

He peed his pants.

Jean Anne stared at him with a frown and shook her head. Then she grinned.

Jean Anne has gotten nastier and nastier toward him over the years. It occurs to him that her nastiness is not just jealousy showing itself but that she maybe sees through him, can look at him and see a soul black with sin.

She knows he is a demon.

TWENTY-TWO

QUEEN FOR A DAY

Samson sits on the sofa in the living room, feeling bloated and exhausted, but he can't go to sleep—he needs to see Ray and then drive to Houston. He just wants to relax a minute.

Mama is watching "Queen for a Day" on the TV, and all of a sudden, Samson finds himself crying. The ladies on the show are all pathetic, brave women. Their husbands are invalids or died or ran out on them, leaving them with five or seven or nine children. The women have had diabetes or cancer or polio; they've lost fingers working in cotton mills; they work two jobs during the day and scrub floors at night; they've been robbed; their children have diabetes or cancer or polio; they have lived in houses in flood zones, in earth quake zones, in tornado alley. But they have survived and been wonderful mothers, and their kids have turned out well, will surely end up being happy, rich doctors and lawyers and scientists and college professors. And these ladies ask for little recognition, just the title of Queen for a Day, a bouquet of roses, a crown, and a new refrigerator or stove or dishwasher. Oh, Lord, Samson can't stop the tears.

"You sick, Daryl?" Mama asks.

He can't talk. He wishes he could save those women, especially the one whose youngest girl was born with a bad hare lip and other deformities that required eighteen operations and who has a pair of very fine hooters.

"Sweetie, you want somethin'? You hungry?"

Samson shakes his head, the tears dropping to his lap. Jesus, what is he thinking of? He can't save even himself.

"You upset 'bout Rachel Marie callin'? She shouldn't ought to be upsetting you."

"Oh, Mama, I been bad." He's just got to get Rachel Marie a dishwasher.

"Did *I* do somethin', Daryl?"

"No, Mama." He chokes on his tears, then hits the arm of the sofa with his fist. He takes a deep breath. He pulls himself together, stops crying. "But you don't listen. I need somebody to talk to. I don't got a single person in my life to talk to. Sometimes I feel like I'm gonna bust with all the stuff I can't tell nobody."

"You should be able to talk to Rachel Marie. And don't you have friends? Some of the other *nice* boys I see on the television wrestlin'?"

"I can't talk to nobody 'bout what I done." He pauses and stares at her. "Mama, I'm gonna go to Hell when I die." But he immediately thinks he's wrong because anybody as full of love as he is can't go to Hell. It wouldn't make sense.

"I taught you to be friendly and make friends with people so long as they weren't trash."

"Let me talk to you, Mama."

"All right. Talk."

He stares at her. Is he crazy? His mama can't help him. She'll say, "I don't believe it," and ask him if he wants her to start fixing lunch.

"Talk."

"Damn it, Mama." He is trying not to cry again.

"Don't cuss. It's trashy."

"I gotta go see Ray."

"Promise you won't cuss," she says, following him to the front door.

"Oh, hell, Mama...."

"Promise."

"I gotta go." He hugs her and kisses her old neck; then he hurries to his Cadillac, limping on his bad foot.

His mama stands on the stoop of the white frame house he recently paid to have painted, waving high in the air one of her thin arms, as he pulls out of the dirt driveway, raising a cloud of red dust.

TWENTY-THREE

BOWLING FOR JESUS

As Samson drives over to the Donie Bowl-O-Rama, the disc jockey on the radio reads the news. The top story is Marilyn Monroe's death. Candy was as upset this morning about Marilyn Monroe as people were when President Roosevelt passed away. Once Samson realized Candy wasn't talking about her friend Marilyn, he lost interest in her grief, but now he, too, feels some shock over the death of such a young and beautiful and famous woman.

The disc jockey mentions that "Marilyn Monroe" wasn't her real name, something Samson never knew. A lot of people aren't who they claim to be: John Wayne, Cary Grant, Rock Hudson—he's heard their names are made up, too. He's not sure about Judy Garland. "Ronald Reagan" sure as hell sounds made up.

Samson wonders whether his own death will get much attention. Some TV announcer will probably just mention his passing between wrestling bouts when he has a couple of seconds to fill after a commercial: *A note here that Samson The Strong Man—some of you might remember him as being a world champion briefly—died recently of a heart attack. Now back to the action.*

That will be all. Most wrestling fans will be in their kitchens getting a snack or going to the bathroom when the news of his death is... mentioned.

Unless you're a movie star or a president, nobody cares much. He still can't believe Hoffman is helping that damn elevator dwarf get into movies. "The gods are pleased, Larry, Curly, and Moe," he says and thinks he sounds wonderful.

Life makes no sense. The race is not always won by the fastest runner—or something like that—the Bible says.

The Donie Bowl-o-Rama is a long low concrete-block building. On the roof is a huge plastic bowling ball full of holes from hail storms. Bowl-o-Rama is out on the edge of town near Skyline Mobile Home Sales, which advertises itself with a mobile home perched in the sky on two one-hundred-and-fifty-foot steel poles. An auto body repair shop nearby has a 1949 Crosley perched on poles high in the air, but it's not as spectacular as the trailer. Every spring the owner of Skyline Mobile Homes has a crew of professional painters refurbish the trailer in the sky. It's a two-tone aqua and white 1952 Skyliner. A somber, black and white sign at the city limits used to announce, "Now entering Donie, Texas, the home of Ernest B. Appleton, U.S. Congressman 1872-1876"; the sign put up seven or eight years ago has red and white letters on a blue background and says, "Welcome to Donie, U.S.A., the home of the trailer in the sky."

In the bowling alley, three ladies are bowling, and a half dozen people sit in the bar. The bowling balls rumbling down the lanes and crashing like thunder into the pins make Samson nervous. He sees Ray at the bar. A woman is perched on the stool next to him, but they're not talking, just drinking. Samson stands back for a moment and studies Ray, who is wearing a striped shirt and black trousers. He looks like a wrestling referee. He's five six and weighs around one-forty, has Mama's bird bones.

When Samson finally goes up to him and says hi, Ray blinks a few times and purposely falls off his stool like a comedian on TV, except nobody laughs; he says to the woman, "Wow! Look here! This is my famous little brother. Daryl. Better known as Simba The Strong Man."

"Who?" The woman makes a face.

"Simba The Strong Man!"

"Samson," Samson mutters.

"Who?" the woman says.

"Who?" Ray says and looks around, waving his arms. "Who? WHO?" He shakes his head. "Do you mean to tell me you have never stayed up past midnight or gotten up at five on Sunday morning to enjoy the fabulous sport and morality play know as professional wrestling? 'The fastest growing sport in America,' according to... to God." He frowns sadly, shakes his head again. His hair has gotten gray all over. He needs a shave, and the stubble on his face is gray, too.

"What the hell are you talkin' about?" The woman's hair is bright red, but her thick eyebrows are coal black.

"It's nice to meet you, ma'am," Samson says, nodding shyly.

"Are you really Ray's brother? What the hell is he talkin' 'bout? You're not a TV preacher, are ya?" She has the bushiest eyebrows he's ever seen on a woman.

"I'm a pro wrestler. That's all."

Ray is lifting a drink to his mouth and spills half of it on his pants. "That's *all*? This man, my brother, my *little* brother, was once champion of the world."

"Really?" The woman looks Samson up and down, gives him a little smile.

"Yes, king of the world." Ray drains his glass, licks his lips. "Shit. Listen, baby, why don't you go shave your under arms or some other hairy spot while I visit with my little brother."

There's a crash of ball and pins. "Strike!" a lady hollers.

"Eat it, Ray," the red-headed woman says.

"Eat it? I did eat it. You loved it. Remember?"

"Eat a fat one."

"Bitch."

"Prick."

"Whore."

"Drunk."

Samson watches the woman sashay away. Although the rest of her isn't very fat, her butt is gigantic. "What's that all about, Ray? I don't want to 'cause trouble between you and your lady friend."

"Naw. We do this all the time. A private joke, little brother. She'll get over it. Want a drink?"

"No, thank you, Ray. I haven't drank a drop since I was in the Navy. Stuff makes me sillier than I am by nature."

"You're a saint. You're a saint. And a big star."

"Ray, now—"

"So you been to see Mama and Jean Anne?"

"Oh, yeah. Mama fixed me a big breakfast."

"I wasn't there. Notice?" Ray takes a drink.

"So how you been doin', Ray?"

Ray shrugs. "Hey, my girl—Helen—what do you think, Daryl?"

"Oh, gosh, she seems real nice. She your steady girl these days?"

Ray never got married and never has had a lot of girlfriends. Samson is thinking that Helen's huge butt could be a character in a science-fiction movie and feels sorry for Ray.

"She's just a bowling fan," Ray says. "You know, there's girls that follow us bowlers all around the country. I met her at a tournament in San Angelo—I got fourth place by the way—and she followed me here. Sucks like a Hoover. It's just like in your business, I'm sure—you got these chicks following you guys around, don't you? You can't tell me Rachel Marie is so good she's all you need."

"Ray, you been drinkin' a lot already this mornin', ain't you?"

"I've had a couple. I'm Goddamn forty-eight years old. I can drink if I want."

"I know. I ain't tryin' to boss you."

"Service! I need some help!" Ray hollers down the bar at the bartender, a big man with rolls of fat at the back of his neck. Samson thinks he looks a little like The Fuhrer. After Ray gets his new drink, he takes a sip, smacks his lips, smiles at Samson, and says, "So tell me, is Rachel Marie a good lay?"

"Ray, you just ain't yourself no more."

"Who is?"

Twenty-five years ago, Ray dated Rachel Marie. That was back when Ray was traveling around the state with a bowling team of Christians who bowled for Jesus and held revivals at bowling alleys. The team went undefeated for three years and saved thousands of souls. Rachel Marie's daddy, Reverend Fuller, thought Ray would be the perfect son-in-law, but Rachel Marie wouldn't marry him. She told him she was waiting for God to give her a sign about her and Ray's relationship and He never did. Ray was crushed. After Samson married Rachel Marie, he asked her once what sign God had given her that made her accept *his* proposal, and she said, "Huh? Sign? What are you talking about?"

Samson stares at the pretty bottles lined up on the shelves behind the bar and asks, "You need any money, Ray?"

Ray takes a drink, clears his throat. "I could accept an offering."

"How much you need?" Samson reaches for his wallet.

"Whatever you can spare without bringing hardship upon yourself and your loved ones."

Samson has ninety dollars in his wallet and gives fifty to Ray, who balls the bills up in his fist and stuffs them into his pants pocket.

"You ever miss preachin'? You were real fine. Stirred the soul, people used to say."

"Oh, I don't know. I got on a lot of people's nerves." He pauses, takes a drink. "Jesus, I was self-righteous. I tried to be like Rachel Marie's old man but didn't have that steel pole for a spine or a rock for a brain. Old Man Fuller never doubted himself or Mr. God once in his life. After he lost half his congregation because of his public accusations, he went right on, doing the same act, never thought of easing up on the poor bastards. And it worked out okay for him. After a while, new people came into the church. You remember. They liked—they *admired*—his rigidness, his pomposity and self-righteousness. Or maybe they just liked the entertainment value of the whole show, the old fart pointing to somebody and screaming, `Adulterer!'"

Ray has gotten loud, and a few other people in the bowling alley bar look at him. Bowling balls thunder like God's wrath.

"Reverend Fuller sure was full of the fire," Samson says softly, nodding.

"He was full of something."

"You still believe in God, don't you?"

"Sure. Can't hurt. Well, it can hurt, but what the hell."

Ray looks old. His face is full of wrinkles. Samson stares at his gray hair.

Ray orders another drink from the bartender, and Samson orders a Dr Pepper. The bartender stays down at the other end of the bar, polishing glasses. Every once in a while, Samson has noticed, he pours himself a drink and turns to the wall to gulp it down. The bar area is closed off from the rest of the bowling alley and is very dimly lit. The thick carpet is the color of dried blood.

Samson doesn't know what to talk about with his own brother. He knows that one of the main reasons Ray left preaching was that his predictions for 1953 didn't come true. Throughout 1952, Ray traveled all over Texas, Oklahoma, New Mexico, and Arkansas, pointing out to congregations that if they added the one, the nine, the five, and the three of 1953 together the total was eighteen, and if they added the sixes of 666 together the total was also eighteen. This fact, along with some verses in the Book of Revelations, led Ray to predict that 1953 was the year of the Anti-Christ, the year of Mr. 666. There would be earth quakes, floods, typhoons, tornadoes, an invasion of locusts, a great war between the world's Christian countries and the Russians and Chinese; the Anti-Christ—the Soviet premier Joseph Stalin—would become ruler of the world. Ray had crowds terrified, but he assured them that it was all part of God's plan—it meant that the time of perfect peace was near; the faithful would soon live in God's house.

Ray told his audiences that he sincerely hoped he was wrong, but as 1953 went along and nothing much happened, he started looking worried. Around Halloween, people started laughing at him. His followers started going in search of a new pastor. Things looked particularly bleak when Stalin died that year. One of Ray's rival preachers started predicting an end to communism in the world in 1956 because twenty-one divided by three was 777. Mama's attitude was no help. She said, "Ray never could do much right." Ray started locking himself in his room at Mama's house with whiskey and beer and wine bottles. While Samson ascended to the top of his profession in 1954, Ray lost everything.

"You got any bowlin' tournaments comin' up soon?" Samson asks.

"Huh? Oh. Yeah, there's one in Dallas in a couple of months. A big one in New Orleans round Christmas. I've never been to New Orleans."

"Between tournaments couldn't you do a little preachin'? I know Mama would like to see you do that."

"I don't live to please Mama. I'm fucking forty-eight years old."

"But you could make a little extra money preachin', couldn't you? You used to make good money."

"You getting tired of giving me handouts? Here. Take your damn money back." But Ray doesn't make a move to dig the fifty dollars out of his pants pocket.

"That ain't what I mean."

Ray turns his head and seems to study the cigarette smoke that has drifted over from the other people in the bar. Samson wonders what happened to Helen. Her eyebrows are about an inch wide.

"You wanta know what the hardest thing is, little brother? You wanta hear this?"

"Sure, Ray. I got a lot of respect for anything you say."

"It wouldn't have been so bad being a flop as a preacher or a lousy pro bowler or a loser with women. I could have handled all that. I mean, most men are losers. I've done and had more than a lot of guys. What's so bad is that I have a brother who's a Goddamn superman."

"What?"

"A superman."

"You gotta stop drinkin' so much, Ray. You're soundin' crazy. If you knew what I really am...."

"I'll tell you what you are. You're Mr. Family Man, Mr. Money Bags, Mr. TV Star—"

"Oh, Ray, you don't know nothin'."

Ray hangs his head, looks down at his lap. When he looks up again, he has tears in his eyes. "You should hear Mama telling people about—"

"Ray, you oughta get your own place to live. You need more than a room at Mama's. You'd feel better if you had your own place. Maybe I—"

Ray starts bawling. He has his elbows on the bar now and his hands over his face. The bartender comes over to them and says to Samson, "Get him outta here."

"What?"

"I don't want none of that shit in here."

Ray holds up a hand, palm out. "It's okay, Bubba. I'm leaving."

Outside, the glare of the sun hurts their eyes. Ray staggers, leans against Samson's Cadillac.

"You want me to take you home? Where's your girl?"

"She's probably in the men's john, doing what she does best."

"Come on. Get in."

"I got my own car. There."

Ray has a 1951 Nash with big rust holes in the fenders and a cracked windshield.

"You'll kill yourself drivin'."

"Don't worry. I won't leave till my head's clear." Ray sits down against the building in the shade of the roof's overhang. "You go on."

"What you doin'? You come on with me now." Samson looks at the flat, brown, empty landscape, the shimmering highway.

"I'll be fine. I'm just gonna rest." Ray buries his face in his folded arms. "Then I'll go home or I'll go back inside. Bubba will let me in. He's just a sentimental guy. Can't stand to see a drunk cry."

"Come on." Samson reaches down and takes Ray's arm, but Ray resists, and Samson lets go. Lord, he's worn out.

"No. You go on."

"No, Ray." Samson squats down to pick him up.

Ray slaps him across the face. "Get the hell out of here! Get the hell away from me. Jesus Christ, you're my little brother." Ray starts crying again. "I used to change your diaper."

"Ray...." Samson stands up, backs off.

"Fuck off. Okay? Just fuck off."

Samson sighs. He squints at the blazing sun. "Okay, Ray." He goes over to his Cadillac and opens the driver's door. Ray has his head hung between his knees.

"You gonna puke?"

Ray shakes his head.

"I love you, Ray."

Ray nods.

Samson gets in his Cadillac and drives away.

TWENTY-FOUR

JAKE THE SNAKE'S BRONZED EAR

A mile or so outside Donie, on the road to Houston, Samson sees Ray's girlfriend waddling along the shoulder in her bare feet, her high heels in her hand. When he's almost right up on her, she turns and extends her free hand, her thumb cocked, her big red purse dangling from her wrist. Her face glows with sweat, and her hair is a mess. Her eyebrows need to be brushed, too.

For the next few miles he thinks about turning back and picking her up. He's not sure why he would, though, and he's sad and exhausted. He imagines her monstrous butt spread across the front seat of his Cadillac, the edge of it touching him. He supposes he'd take her back to Bowl-o-Rama. Ray surely needs a woman. But he doesn't need one like her.

Samson drives on.

He has all the windows down and the radio loud to keep him awake. The highway is wavy like a mirage.

In the middle of the afternoon, although he doesn't usually stop for meals along the stretch between Donie and Houston, he pulls off at a restaurant. His idea is that food can make up for a lack of sleep. The name of the place is The

Lonely Star Cafe. A big sign says, "Truckers welcome," and behind the cafe, there's a long concrete-block building with a sign that says, "Come Clean—Showers 50 cents."

At the entrance of the concrete-block building there's a supply room and a window where Samson hands two quarters to the attendant, a young guy who reminds him of Iron Man Mike except that his head is a normal size— not too small for the rest of him. The attendant gives him a little bar of soap and a towel worn thin. Samson stays in the shower a long time, and it helps, makes him a little less worn out and more alert. On the walls opposite the shower stalls are mirrors and sinks and condom machines (French ticklers 25 cents, regular rubbers 10 cents).

When he returns the towel, the attendant says, "You look like you could use a woman."

Samson knows truck stops well. He catches on right away that the shower attendant is a pimp. "A woman is the last thing I need," Samson mutters.

He hates whores. He thinks again of Ray's girlfriend, wonders whether she's an actual professional or just a semi-pro. It's sad to think a man would pay for her. But some men can't be picky, or they have strange tastes. When Samson was with The Baldwin Circus and Carnival, there were always a lot of farmers and soda jerks and deputy sheriffs in the small towns who paid to screw The Fat Lady, a hideous thing—"639 pounds of woman," her posters said. You could barely see her eyes.

He goes inside the cafe and sits in a big booth instead of on a stool at the counter so that he can stretch out and be comfortable. The menu is greasy. The waitress comes over with her order pad and pencil, and he orders a salad, a T-bone steak, a baked potato, grits, green beans, and buttermilk. He eats all the bread in the bread basket before his salad comes.

The waitress is a thin, flat-chested young girl, pale and sad looking, dark circles under her eyes. Her belly pooches out some, but Samson can't tell whether she has poor muscle tone or is in the early stages of pregnancy. She doesn't have a ring on her finger. He feels sorry for her, would like to adopt her. He plans to leave her a five-dollar tip.

It's a slow time, too early for the evening rush, and only one other customer is in the place, a trucker sitting at the counter. The trucker keeps glancing over at him. Samson ignores him and concentrates on his food until the trucker comes over to him and says, "Hey, ain't you... or didn't you used to be...." He's wagging his finger at Samson. "Used to be one of them pro wrestler guys on TV?" The man is wiry and has a long thin face and small eyes. There are wide streaks of grease on both legs of his denim trousers. He wears a red cap with greasy finger prints on the bill.

Samson grins, his mouth full of tough, sinewy T-bone steak, nods his head.

"Me and my cousin are big wrestlin' fans. You're Samson the Strong Man, ain't ya? I used to think you was real good. Why'd you quit?"

Shaking his head, Samson swallows. "I didn't quit."

"I ain't seen you on TV in years."

"I'm on in Houston mostly."

"I live in Houston. You ever think of makin' a comeback?"

"Like I just said—"

"I'll tell you who else I like. That Jake The Snake. He's one mean son of a bitch. My cousin met him one time—in a bar in Potosi—and Jake The Snake invited him over to his house. My cousin said it was like a palace. Said he—. Hey, didn't ole Jake chop off your ear back a few years ago?"

Samson continues eating, keeps his eyes on his food.

"Did it grow back?"

Samson looks up at the man, who is leaning on the table, leaning close to him. The man seems to be entirely serious.

"I hear Jake keeps your ear on his fireplace mantle like a trophy. Had it bronzed. Boy, ain't that a hoot?" The trucker straightens up and cackles.

"That ain't true," Samson says, staring at his grits.

"What?"

"It ain't true what you heard. He don't have my ear. It was just part of my ear, and he don't have it."

"My cousin's been in the man's house. My cousin wouldn't lie. Not 'bout a thing like that."

"Jake don't have it." Samson doesn't know what happened to the top of his ear. He was taken to the hospital right away. Some janitor probably swept it up and threw it in the trash. "He don't have it," Samson says softly, thinking how he should have killed Jake's Goddamn dogs.

"Well, I don't cotton none to you callin' my cousin a liar, even if you did used to be my second favorite wrestler after Jake The Snake."

The little flat-chested waitress comes up and says to Samson, "Can I get you anything else, sir?"

"No, thank you. Appreciate it."

The trucker looks the girl up and down and says, "I could use a little sugar and honey," and pinches her behind.

Then Samson finds himself standing over the guy. He doesn't know exactly what happened. The trucker is lying on the floor all twisted up, blood flowing out of his nose. The waitress is staring wide-eyed at Samson and screaming.

"That son of a bitch," Samson mumbles.

"He's my boyfriend!" she sobs.

Samson steps toward her to give her a hug, but stops himself when she whips out her stubby pencil and makes like she intends to stab him with it. The waitress drops to her knees beside the trucker, who's groaning now and trying to sit up. The waitress cradles his bloody head in her lap.

Blood roars in Samson's brain, and he tosses all the money he has—about forty dollars—on the table and gets out of there.

He drives fast for a while, his adrenaline pumping. He keeps looking in the rearview mirror for highway-patrol cars.

After about an hour, he figures nobody called the police and he starts to relax some.

Then he's more exhausted than ever. His chest hurts. Heart burn or heart attack—he's too tired to care much. He has a headache. He keeps belching. His teeth ache from chewing the tough steak.

Finally, he pulls onto the shoulder of the road and closes his eyes. Just a nap. Ten minutes maybe.

When he wakes up, it's four in the morning.

TWENTY-FIVE

HOME

Houston, Texas

When he's nearly to Rachel Marie's, he remembers dreaming about Buddy Hoffman and the trucker he punched at The Lonely Star. Something blurry and wild happened, all in vivid movie colors, Technicolor, but Samson can't recall exactly what.

Samson passes the Piggly Wiggly where Rachel Marie grocery shops, the neighborhood post office built just last year, the community swimming pool surrounded by a high chain-link fence, the elementary school with its big American flag flying out front (not even Marilyn Monroe rates putting it at half mast; a person has to be an astronaut or president to get that). He turns down his street and thinks how he used to call this place "home." Now it's where Rachel Marie and the boys live—Samson has no home. This used to be his real life. Now he has no real life.

His neighbors are leaving for work. Dressed up in business suits, they avoid their lawn sprinklers. They give him snobby looks or ignore him as he passes their houses. Samson thinks about how his Cadillac is the nicest car on the block. His neighbors have Pontiacs, Buicks, Chevy Impalas.

Rachel Marie, Earl, Benny Bob, and Daryl Junior live in an all-brick two-story house with air conditioning. The house is surrounded by shrubs and trees and other nice houses, and their neighbors are accountants, lawyers, grocery-store managers, chiropractors, and even a dentist three houses down—good people (voters, school-board members, charity-drive chairmen), although they're snobs and seldom wave back when Samson waves. They probably think he's a freak—a huge man weighing nearly three hundred pounds with hair down to his shoulders; they just aren't friendly, even though Samson and his family have lived here eight years and don't have wild parties and Rachel Marie keeps the grass mowed and the shrubs trimmed. Nevertheless, he has always hoped the nice neighborhood and house will help his boys grow up to be happy and good.

He parks in the driveway next to Rachel Marie's black and white Ford Falcon station wagon. There are two wrecked cars in the garage. The '55 Chevy has a crumpled grill and hood, a smashed head light, and a busted radiator. The '49 Mercury has deep gashes the entire length of the passenger's side. Two other cars Daryl Junior has wrecked were total loses. Daryl Junior likes to pretend he's a race-car driver, and he doesn't seem to understand what a red light means. Last month, a judge took away his driver's license until he turns eighteen.

When Samson opens the front door, the house is cool and smells like pine air freshener. In the kitchen, Rachel Marie is buttering hot corn muffins for Earl and Benny Bob. Daryl Junior is not in sight. The boys spring out of their chairs, leap onto their daddy, and he hugs them fiercely, squeezes them. Oh, God, the love he feels. His heart is bursting. Tears come to his eyes, his throat hurts. After a minute, he lets them go and manages to tell them he has Flintstone glasses in his car, and they run out to get them. Rachel Marie gives him a peck on the cheek, keeps buttering a muffin.

"I'm real sorry 'bout bein' late," Samson says as he sits down at the kitchen table. "I pulled off the road to nap a little and ended up sleepin' near all night."

"It's all right," she says as she takes a whole chicken out of the refrigerator. Then she stretches on her tip toes to get a big knife from a high cabinet the boys can't reach. "I figured it was something like that."

Her simple statement causes sadness to wash over him. Years ago she would have called the highway patrol and asked about accidents, then filed a missing-person report. She would have been crying when he finally got home. It's obvious that she doesn't love him as much as she used to. He feels tears come to his eyes. She starts cutting up the chicken, and he watches her narrow back, notices for the ten thousandth time the way her shoulder blades poke out, look sharp under her thin blouse.

"Buddy Hoffman called yesterday," she says.

Samson takes a bite of one of the boys' corn muffins. The butter tastes a little rancid. "Yeah? What he say?"

"Not much."

"Oh."

"You need to call him."

"Okay." Samson watches her continue to mutilate the chicken. Is this the way she would react to finding out what he really is—a monster and a son of a bitch—not look at him and mutilate a chicken?

Earl and Benny Bob run in, each holding a Flintstone glass and tell their mother they want Kool Aid.

"I'll have to wash those glasses first."

"Wash them now," Earl says.

"You don't boss your mama, boy," Samson says.

"It's okay," Rachel Marie says, running water in the sink.

"You spoil them silly."

"You're the one that brought them the glasses."

"Yeah, well.... Where's Daryl Junior? He still asleep?"

"No."

"He didn't stay over at that Slatter boy's house last night, did he? Those Slatters are pure trash."

"He got a job."

"He what? He got a job?" Samson grins, watches Rachel Marie take some more corn muffins out of the oven. "I thought he decided a summer job was a waste of time. Interfered with more important things, like listenin' to the radio and watchin' TV and wreckin' cars."

"Well, he got one. He's washing cars at Al's Used Car Lot. He thinks he can get on as a mechanic after a while." She sets a plate of six corn muffins in front of Samson and pours him a cup of coffee.

"Al Lewis is the biggest crook in Texas. What's Daryl Junior gonna do? Learn how to turn back odometers? Fill crank cases with saw dust?" He eats a corn muffin in one bite. The butter is definitely rancid.

"We'll talk about it later," Rachel Marie says, nodding at Earl and Benny Bob, who are sitting at the table and studying the Flintstone characters stenciled on their glasses. "You can finish your muffins and then go take a shower."

"Is this Daryl Junior's first day on the job? If he wants to work, there's—"

"We'll talk about it."

Samson sighs. He wishes he knew what the hell was going on. He watches Rachel Marie roll the chicken parts in flour and her own special seasoning. Maybe her not talking much and her not looking at him are the result of nothing except seventeen years of marriage. He can't remember the last time she acted really glad to see him. After seventeen years—hell, a lot quicker than that—you get used to a person and that person is like a part of you, like one of your toes or your liver or your heart, a part you don't pay much attention to until it hurts you. In seventeen years, Candy will be indifferent to his arrivals and departures—Jesus, he wonders, will he still be wrestling? How? It will be 1979. He will be sixty. More likely he will be dead.

He eats all the muffins, despite the rancid butter, and Rachel Marie pours him more coffee.

"Hoffman wants me to call him, huh?"

"Uh huh."

"He didn't say nothin' else?"

"Not really. He asked how the boys and I were. He was nice."

"I'll call him from upstairs."

He stands and heads out but pauses in the doorway and looks at her profile. She looks like a schoolmarm, something prim and pinched about her face—not ugly though, not exactly—the kind of teacher who cracks kids' knuckles, not the kind that would spoil children with Kool Aid early in the morning.

She is a mystery. Then again, who isn't? He almost tells her that Ray says hi, but that's not really true, so he goes on upstairs, his legs aching from too many bouts for too many years, from too many women and not enough sleep.

He sits on the edge of his and Rachel Marie's king-sized solid-oak four-poster bed, and from the drawer in the night stand, he takes a tin box he keeps cash in. The box contains sixty-two dollars and fourteen cents. Also in the night stand are unpaid bills from All-State auto insurance, South Texas Electric, New York Life, and Liberty Mortgage. "Jesus Christ," he whispers. He rubs his forehead.

On the floor by the bed he notices a package addressed to him. He shakes it and it sounds like a box of gravel. After he opens the box, he stares, trying to figure out what exactly he's looking at. The box is full of plastic model pieces. There are dozens of little wagon wheels. Then he remembers that six months ago he sent away for the Borax Mule Team wagon train Ronald Reagan talked about on TV on "Death Valley Days." The instructions Samson finds at the bottom of the box look like the blue prints for a jet. Samson has no idea how he will put the thing together. His ability to concentrate is shot these days.

Finally, he picks up the white Princess phone he got Rachel Marie a couple of years ago because she thought it was so much prettier than normal black phones, and dials Hoffman's office.

"Hoffman, I hear you called my wife."

"Listen, Daryl. Everything's set for Mexico. The animal protection laws down there are nothing."

"You listen, Hoffman—" But he doesn't really have anything to say.

"Daryl? You still there?"

Samson sighs and almost whispers, "Yeah."

"Your wife sounds like a real nice lady."

"What you tryin' to pull?"

"Listen, about Mexico. You'll be glad to hear this. You'll get an extra five thousand pesos per match."

"Huh?"

"Lots of Pesos."

"Yeah, but—"

"Come in next week on your way through Dallas, and we'll talk. Sign the contracts and all."

He's staring at the picture over the bed: a worn-out old cowboy on a horse. "What I got to do with the animals?"

"It's just going to be a burrow probably."

"How 'bout a movie contract? I can lose some weight if my belly's a problem. I can get a wig. I can—"

"See you next week, okay, Daryl? I've got an appointment that just arrived." Hoffman hangs up on him.

Samson goes into the bathroom and takes four aspirins and turns on the shower. He stares at the bathtub and thinks about filling it with hot water, then sinking down in it and opening his veins with a razor blade. He shudders. He can't stand the sight of his own blood.

After he showers, he spends a few minutes dabbing hair-growing tonic on his scalp. Drinking this stuff would be a strange way of killing himself. Hair growing in his gut, on his tongue, in his throat.

Then looking at his face in the mirror, he prays: "Please, Lord, don't ever let Rachel Marie find out 'bout what I been doin'. Please, God. I'll be good for now on. I'll change."

TWENTY-SIX

THE REFRIGERATOR

As he starts down the stairs, Samson imagines walking into the kitchen and saying, "Well, darlin', you wanted to talk. You said we had trouble."

And Rachel Marie says, "Talk? Trouble? I just missed you." She turns away from the sink and hugs him hard, stands on her tip toes so they can kiss.

God can do that kind of thing—make everything all right, make everything perfect.

Then Samson imagines walking into the kitchen and saying, "Well, darlin'—"

And Rachel Marie turns around with the knife she was using on the chicken and shoves it into his fat gut....

God is vengeful. God works in strange ways. Fact is you never know what the hell He's going to do.

When he gets to the bottom of the stairs, he decides not to go into the kitchen yet but to look in on the boys. Earl and Benny Bob are in the family room, watching some clown show on TV. Samson pats their heads. Then the show catches his attention.

For a second, he could swear the clown is the one he caught with his first wife, but that was twenty-five years ago and far off, way up north, and that guy wasn't stocky like this one or.... "What you call this show you're watchin'?" he asks the boys.

"'The Uncle Ed Show,'" they both answer at the same time.

The clown has a studio full of kids and their mamas. The clown asks some of the kids what they want to be when they grow up. Policeman. Fireman. Baseball player. One kid says he wants to marry his mommy. Samson looks at his boys. Earl always says he wants to dig up dinosaurs. Benny Bob always tells people he wants to be a professional wrestler.

After the kids on the TV tell the clown what they want to grow up to be, he gives them suckers. He gives one of the mamas a couple of suckers, too. A blonde with nice hooters, kind of looks like poor dead Marilyn Monroe.

Then the clown sings a song: "Put your toys away, don't delay, help your mommy have a happy day...."

Samson wonders how many of those kids will grow up sad and mean, robbing banks and killing people in 1985, 1990, 2000—robbing banks on Mars.

He listens to the clown's Yankee accent. Son of bitch. Samson is stunned. It is that clown. Eddie Buckles.

Fuck.

Samson stands there in the family room until the show is over and learns that it's syndicated out of Chicago. Son of a bitch. The clown probably makes a bundle. He had his clown make-up on when Samson caught him with Macy. For some reason, that make-up was why Samson couldn't hit him in the face. He recalls the sickening sound of ribs cracking. Then he went after Macy and there was the sound of nose cartilage cracking. He sees blood all over Macy's face. He has no idea whatever became of her. He loved her, and she broke his heart. Now she's old and fat, probably. Like him.

He pats his boys' heads again. "I love you fellahs," he says.

In the kitchen, Rachel Marie appears to be waiting for him. She's sitting at the table, drinking tea. Clean dishes drip in the plastic drainer on the counter. Lord, he needs to get her a dishwasher. She's a good woman, even if she doesn't seem to love him anymore.

He sits down. "Yeah?"

"It's Daryl Junior."

"Daryl Junior? What else besides that?"

"It's just Daryl Junior. What do you mean?"

"Nothin'. I don't know." Relief mixes with fear for his oldest boy, who's going to send him to an early grave for sure. "What 'bout him? He didn't get hold of somebody's car, did he?"

"He... well, he got that little girlfriend of his.... She's going to have a baby." Her face shatters with grief, showing her age, and her tears pour. She leans toward him, and he scoots his chair over to her so that she can cry on his shoulder.

Samson has to work hard to remember Daryl Junior's girlfriend. Being on the road so much he doesn't see his family enough. "That little girl? What's her name? Jesus Christ."

"You don't have to swear."

"Shit, woman." He shrugs his shoulder, and she lifts her head up.

"Daryl—" She gives him a hard look. "Now, Daryl—"

"I'm sorry." He looks at a box of salt on the counter by the refrigerator. A girl holds an umbrella over her head. *When it rains it pours.* "I just can't believe he'd do somethin' so stupid."

Rachel Marie nods and cries. She blows her nose hard on a napkin. A big horn. A fat man's fart.

She's probably as thankful as she can be that her old man is dead, Samson figures. It's been five years since Reverend Fuller keeled over one Sunday morning just as he aimed his long finger at a church elder who had his wife and five kids sitting beside him. Everybody in church that day said the elder let out a huge sigh of relief as Reverend Fuller turned purple and stopped breathing.

"She ain't but his age, is she?"

"She's a year younger."

"She's fifteen?"

"Yes."

Samson shakes his head. He recalls that Tammy Sue White was only fourteen when he screwed her in the stock room of his daddy's hardware store. But that was different. He's not sure how, but when he has time, he'll figure it out.

"I'll kill that boy."

"They're going to get married."

"Like hell."

"Next Saturday. At her parents' house. They told me and her parents three days ago. I tried to call you at your motel in Oklahoma City, but they said you hadn't stayed there in months."

"I been tryin' out some of the new motels. I should of told you. I forgot. I should of called more, too, I know. I just—"

"You'll be here next Saturday, won't you?"

"Can't the girl just go away somewhere for a few months? Ain't there homes?"

"Would you want your first grandchild put up for adoption?"

Grandchild. He hasn't thought of the baby as his grandchild. He is going to be a granddaddy.

"So? Are you?"

"What?"

"Going to be here next Saturday?"

He nods, reaches over and takes Rachel Marie's hands in his big hairy paws. They sit there like that for a few minutes, looking at nothing. It's the first grief in their lives they've shared equally. He grieved more when his daddy died. Her grief was greater when hers died. Now they have something to truly share.

"How they gonna live?"

"They'll stay with us."

"So I get all the baby bills, and I feed his face and hers, too."

"He's got that job now. At least he's taking some responsibility."

"Washin' cars." Samson shakes his head. "I reckon he's not goin' back to school."

"I told him I wanted him to, but he says he just wants to work on cars, so he doesn't see any point."

"All he knows how to do is wreck 'em. He tried to replace the brake pads on that Oldsmobile I got him for his birthday and he plowed into the back of a milk truck."

Samson looks around the shiny kitchen, at the pine cabinets, the sink, the stove, that box of salt, and the big white refrigerator.

He focuses on the refrigerator as if it were to blame for this mess Daryl Junior's gotten into. That damn refrigerator should have prevented this kind of thing.

TWENTY-SEVEN

SAMSON'S HEART

Samson sits in his leather lounge chair in the sunken family room, wanting to be with his littlest boys. Although he and Rachel Marie never use it, there's a fireplace in the family room. One wall has built-in book shelves, on which Rachel Marie keeps her Reader's Digest condensed books. The floor is covered with wall-to-wall carpet, brownish orange stuff that's thick, stain resistant, and expensive. The ceiling plaster has tiny flakes of gold in it. *All this!* Samson thinks, and Daryl Junior turns out to be white trash.

Samson watches Earl and Benny Bob color pictures of dinosaurs. They're lying in front of the TV, their crayons working furiously. They're making the dinosaurs purple and green and red. "To Tell the Truth" is on; two of three ladies are lying about being members of an Austrian royal family. One is wearing a tiara covered in diamonds (or what look like diamonds). The other two have on dresses, look like ordinary women, maybe secretaries or bank tellers or school teachers. The real princess will be one of the ordinary-looking ones, Samson would bet. He watches his boys color dinosaurs, thinking there is still maybe hope for his babies—if he changes, if he becomes an honest man. Earl and Benny Bob could still turn out all right. It's too late for Daryl Junior, though. God has picked this way of punishing Samson.

He can turn his head and see into the kitchen where Rachel Marie is frying chicken, and he thinks about how stuffed with love his heart is for that frail woman and these boys.

Why—if he loves this family so much—does he have Darlene and Candy?

He feels an impulse to walk into the kitchen and tell Rachel Marie how much he loves her and loves the way she has cooked and cleaned and cared for him and his boys all these years. But if he does that, won't he be a hypocrite? Won't he be a fake?

Should he tell her the truth then about what he's been doing the last couple of years? No, the truth would be the cruelest thing he could inflict on her. She would die of grief and shame.

Then again, maybe she wouldn't care much. She doesn't love him now the way she used to. God gave her no sign when Ray proposed, and He didn't give her one when Samson did either, but maybe she was getting scared of being an old maid. Maybe she faked love for years but now can't keep it up. One thing Samson knows for sure—he has never faked love.

She was everything Samson was looking for when he returned to Texas after the war. He had gotten into wrestling right away—Stan Edwards said he had tremendous potential. Every time he passed through Donie, Samson visited Mama and Jean Anne. (Ray, who had been rejected for military service because of his flat feet, was always on the road with his Christian bowling team—"Every strike," he said, "is a strike against Satan!") One Sunday in the fall of 1945, Samson was in Donie and went to church with Mama and Jean Anne, and there Rachel Marie was, prettier than he remembered from when Ray had dated her in '41. She had filled out slightly, although she still had little birdy breasts and that pinched look to her face. But she was what he wanted, he realized, or at least what he needed—a sweet Christian woman who could cook and who would be faithful to him. He wanted nothing to do with phony blondes who could swallow three-foot swords or with smelly, lazy whores like the ones he met in Navy towns. "Port holes," the sailors called the whores.

After all those years of being a faithful husband, what happened to him?

One thing, he did get lonely away from home. The hotel and motel rooms were always painted some sick pink or green or yellow; there was never enough light—he could barely read the newspaper. He could hear people in other rooms coughing and puking and laughing and screwing. The sounds of screwing were the worst.

He was alone and needed a woman, but not just a whore. You could still be lonely as hell with a naked woman beside you if she was a whore. After fifteen years of lonely nights on the road he guesses something in him just snapped.

He thinks hard now to come up with a better theory.

Well, another reason was that maybe he wanted to be kind of born again, to start over, to be young again by starting another family.

That explains Darlene better than it does Candy, who is just something he missed when he was twenty. Then he shakes his head vehemently.

"Why you shakin' your head?" Earl asks. He gets no answer.

No, Candy isn't just something he missed when he was young. After all, he had Macy, who had a fine body and special... talents.

He loves Candy, loves her deeply. It is not just her ways in bed that have a hold on him. There's something... spiritual. Yes, something about her touches his—

He tries to think of other explanations for turning bad. Of course a man got tired of his wife's body after so many years and....

Earl is standing between Samson's legs, his hands on Samson's knees, saying, "Daddy, Daddy."

Samson turns his head and stares into the kitchen at Rachel Marie. He is tired of her in bed maybe, but he loves her more now than ever.

"Why are you movin' your head like that?"

Samson looks at Earl. "Huh?" Earl is frail like Rachel Marie.

"Like this." The child shakes his head furiously, then nods furiously.

"I was just thinkin'."

Benny Bob is sneaking up on Earl. Twice as big as Earl, he has his daddy's frame and a Mohawk haircut. He started insisting when he was three that he had his career as a professional wrestler all figured out. He is going to be Big Indian Ben and scalp his opponents. Samson asked him once what he was going to do with the scalps, and Benny Bob said, "I'll give 'em to pretty girls and they'll kiss me for 'em."

"Watch out, Earl," Samson says, just as Benny Bob grabs him from behind, throws him to the floor, and gets on top of him. He grabs Earl's hair, and Earl screams.

While the boys wrestle, Samson looks again in the direction of the kitchen. Rachel Marie is turning over the popping, sizzling chicken. He keeps staring at her while Benny Bob hits Earl on the head with a rubber tomahawk. Rachel Marie has the scrawniest butt, Samson thinks. He used to joke about it when he was with a bunch of wrestlers in a locker room or in a gym lifting weights or playing poker sometimes at Bobo Brazil's house in Dallas (his life now has no room for even the few friends he used to have); he'd say she was built like the cartoon character Gumby, flat in front and flat in back, insisting he loved the sweet woman anyway; other men could have their fat sluts. Her butt isn't something to joke about these days. That scrawny behind makes him kind of sad for some reason. Then he thinks about Candy's smooth, round bottom. He hates himself for loving her butt. In a few seconds, though, he starts hating Rachel Marie for having a scrawny butt.

Earl is crying, "Daddy! Make him stop!" Benny Bob is hooting and yelping like an Indian on the warpath.

Then Samson hates Candy for having that awfully fine bottom. Whose fault is it that he's a son of a bitch? And what about Darlene's butt? In her case, it's more her big tits that are the issue.

"Daddy! Make him stop!"

All of a sudden, damn it, if he isn't getting excited right here—all these thoughts of tits and butts—with his littlest boys playing at his feet.

"Daddy!"

"Goddamn it, go play somewhere else!" Samson roars.

The boys stop struggling and stare at him. "We—" Benny Bob starts to say.

"Go on! Get the hell out of here 'fore I whip your behinds. Go play in the street."

Earl says, "Why you all red?"

"Get!" Samson screams. "Get the Goddamn hell out!"

They run out of the room and out the front door into the scorching Houston heat. Samson's chest is heaving. Sweat trickles down his temples. They must be scared to run like that. Jesus, he is a monster. Running off to get girls pregnant. What can you expect from boys with a daddy like him.

Rachel Marie is standing in the doorway leading from the kitchen, her eyes shiny and angry, her lips pursed.

He can't look at her. He is furious with love and pity and hate for her. He has to get out.

TWENTY-EIGHT

THE WRATH OF GOD

Samson is in the locker room of Sam Houston Arena, trying to squeeze into his Samson The Strong Man outfit. The thing must have shrunk. Several rows of lockers away Steve Stevens and Pete "The Meat Man" Mason are playing poker; they'll be wrestling each other in the first match tonight. The second match on the bill is Fox Smith and Studs Manly. Samson and Tonga The African Wild Man are the opponents in the finale, a Texas Cage Death Match.

In Sam Houston Arena, Samson has fought hundreds of bouts over the years; he defeated The Sheik for the world championship here (all over the arena billboards advertising the match said "The Sheik vs. Bobby Shine" with Shine's name crossed out and "Samson The Strong Man" written in with red crayon). Immediately after the referee declared Samson the winner, Stan Edwards climbed into the ring and presented Samson The Strong Man with the world championship belt. The Sheik was still in the ring, too, passed out and surrounded by eight wailing wives. The crowd roared for Samson as he wrapped the belt around his waist (thirty-five inches back then). They loved him. They loved him, it seemed, as much as they had ever loved Bobby Shine. Out in the parking lot one of The Sheik's wives was waiting for Samson by his Buick. She asked him out for a drink, but he told her that he didn't drink and that he had to get home to his pregnant wife.

Samson finally manages to struggle into his costume, but it binds and bites and pinches his flesh in several places. He looks down at his huge belly and belches, tasting again the greasy chili he had at Hot Helen's Chili Parlor near the arena. He had three bowls, then ran out of money.

Samson had already given a twenty-dollar bill to a wino sprawled against an old building muttering, "I'm dyin'. I'm dyin'. I ain't ate nothin' in a week." Other people on the street walked right on by, but Samson stopped and looked down at the guy. He didn't know why, but he wanted to kick him. Then he felt guilty for wanting to kick him and dropped the twenty onto the wino's chest. "Jesus loves ya, sir," the wino said. "Jesus loves ya."

Samson hears the slap of playing cards and Steve Stevens say, "Shiiiiittttttt!" and Pete "The Meat Man" Mason cackle.

Samson gave more money this afternoon to a little girl in a dirty dress sitting on the stoop of a narrow, two-family house. She was about six and had dirty, stringy hair. Her nose ran. Her knees were grimy and had scabs on them. Inside the house, a woman was screeching, "I hope you wake up dead! Dead, you hear me! You son of a bitch! Dead! I want you dead!"

A man shouted, "You don't give me orders, bitch. You can't cook, you can't clean, you can't fuck. Why should I—"

"Dead! You're one dead mother fucker! You won't wake up in the mornin'."

The man laughed—long and deep, then started coughing and couldn't stop.

Glass shattered—a bottle maybe or a mirror.

The little girl had her hands pressed over her ears and her eyes closed and was singing Ricky Nelson's song "I'm a Traveling Man" as loud as she could in her sad, desperate little-girl voice. When she realized someone was standing near her and she opened her eyes and saw Samson, she stopped singing, but her mouth stayed open. She had probably never seen a two-hundred and ninety-pound man with long hair. Samson smiled at her.

"Dead! You mother fucker!" the woman inside the house shouted.

The man said, "You sorry sack of shit."

Both of them sounded drunk.

Samson wanted to snatch up the little girl and carry her off to one of his homes where he'd give her good meals and pink dresses with bows and lace and fancy dolls and her own record player.

Something else shattered inside the house.

Samson asked the little girl her name, but she wouldn't answer him. She just stared up at him from the stoop. Samson was thinking that he could steal her and give her to Candy. But he knew he was being silly. He felt tears well up. He took out his wallet and handed the girl several bills— he didn't count how much. He wanted to tell her how to spend it: Campbell's soup, milk, Hershey's bars. But a fat woman with no front teeth burst out the screen door, letting it bang behind her. Her eyes were wide, the whites of them bright in her purple face. Her arms swung in circles, her fists clenched. "What the hell you doin' with my girl? I seen you out here eyeballin' my baby."

He glanced down at the girl. She had stashed the money away somewhere.

"I'll call the cops, you fat pervert. Come on, Trace Lynn. Get away from that man."

Samson held up his hands, his palms out, and backed away. He stumbled on a piece of brick.

When he went into the chili parlor for supper, he had only two dollars. Now, here in the locker room at Sam Houston Arena, it's been only an hour since he ate, but he's starting to feel hungry again.

"Dad."

Samson is startled, turns quickly.

"Daryl Junior. What you doin' here?"

Daryl Junior's hair is black, brushed back like Elvis Presley's. He's about five-six and weighs around one thirty-five—another child in which Samson's genes have lost out (thank the Lord for Benny Bob).

"Mom said you were acting like a maniac at home and left before dinner."

"She send any chicken with you?"

"No."

"Oh." If she still loved him the way she used to, she would have sent chicken.

"Mary's out in the hall."

"Who?"

"*Mary.* You know, my girlfriend. My fiancee."

Fiancee is a funny French word that sounds a little obscene to Samson, like most French words.

"Well, let's go meet her," Samson says. "But first I want a hug from my boy."

"Oh, come off it, Dad." Daryl Junior backs up, chuckles but also looks terrified.

"Guess you're a man now." Samson grabs the little trouble maker and hugs him anyway.

Mary is a shy, skinny girl. Maybe she reminded Daryl Junior of Rachel Marie. Her hair and eyebrows are pale yellow. She wears no make-up. Her eyes are brownish-gray. She has almost no hips, and Samson wonders how in the world a baby will live and grow in that narrow space.

Samson says hi, and she says hi. Samson sticks out his big paw for her to shake, and she stares at it a moment, her eyes round and confused and scared, until she understands. Her hand is small and soft and wet. Then they both avoid eye contact, and both keep glancing at Daryl Junior, expecting him to take charge of the situation, lead the conversation, but he seems to be checking out a couple of slutty-looking girls with four sailors down at the other end of the hall.

Mary's wearing a white dress with small pink flowers all over it, her calves chop sticks, her knees knobby, her breasts pencil erasers. She looks like the little-girl virgin she should be.

"You gonna stay and watch my match?" Samson asks.

"I think so," Mary says, looking at Daryl Junior.

Daryl Junior is still watching the slutty girls with the sailors. One of the sailors has a transistor radio, and the two girls do a couple of dance steps to the tinny music while the sailors ogle them. Daryl Junior grins.

"Daryl, you stayin'?" Samson asks. "Daryl?"

Daryl Junior looks at Samson and says, "Benny Bob and Earl said you were actin' real weird and cussed at them, then ran out of the house just when Mom was gettin' your dinner."

"Well, yeah, I, ah, had to—I all of a sudden—" Then Samson realizes he doesn't need to make excuses, to explain his actions to his son. Good God, the boy is the one who should be explaining a few things. Rock 'n Roll music makes kids bad.

"I figured you got mad after Mom told you about me and Mary."

Rock 'n Roll.

Phony lying fathers, too.

"Your mama says you're gettin' married next Saturday." Samson looks at Mary, whose face turns almost scarlet, an unhealthy color, and he wonders whether she's sick. "Mary, I'd like to meet your mama and daddy sometime." Her people should have taught their daughter some morals. If Tina Lee ever—

"Yes, sir." Her voice is fragile, glasses tinkling as you touch them together.

"You'll *meet* them next Saturday," Daryl Junior says as if his daddy is a moron.

Samson glares at him. "I'd like to meet them before."

"Why?"

Samson's right arm flinches as he has to restrain himself from smacking Daryl Junior. "What's this about you workin' at Al's Used Cars?"

"It's not bad. I'm just doin' clean up now, but I'm gonna train to be a mechanic."

"You know that guy Al ain't what he says. He gets on the television and acts like he's everybody's friend, like he's going to just *give away* these great used cars that barely got any mileage on 'em. He's the biggest phony round. I know for a fact he rolls back odometers."

"He drives a Cadillac just like yours."

"That don't mean he ain't a crook. I'd just like to see you finish school. I was gonna send you to college. I thought you wanted to be a dentist."

"Yeah, when I was nine years old. Where the hell have you been?"

Samson nods. His anger is gone, replaced by pure sadness. His boy—a grease monkey. Samson's fault: sinful, weak, never home.

God is punishing him through his boy. Samson remembers a little boy who stole nails and a hammer from Daddy's store to build a play house. The boy stole lumber from a lumber yard. He was also known to steal hard candies from the drug store. When the boy's mother died of cancer a few months later, the boy blamed himself because he was a thief—Reverend Fuller had explained such things. Before he was twenty the boy became a worthless drunk.

The wrath of God.

Mary is looking at her feet.

"Him being a grease monkey okay with you?" Samson asks her.

She shrugs, keeps her eyes on her feet.

He looks at her shiny patent-leather shoes. Samson's daughter-in-law. He's going to be a granddaddy. He looks at the blank wall behind her, then at her belly. A granddaddy. A valve in his heart opens, and new, warm blood flows through it.

"Want a cigarette?" Daryl Junior asks.

"Huh?" Samson is startled to see his son holding a pack of Camels out to him. The boy knows his daddy doesn't smoke. Camels—Buddy Hoffman's brand.

"When you start smokin'?"

"Long time ago."

The boy is showing off. For him? For the girl? "You know I don't smoke, boy."

Daryl Junior shrugs, puts his pack of Camels back in his shirt pocket, and smiles at Mary, who frowns and blushes again.

Good Lord, Daryl Junior—his first born (except maybe for the half Martian in Nebraska)—is smoking and screwing.

"Mary's never seen you wrestle."

"You gonna stay and watch?"

"Yeah."

"I heard you're very good," Mary says meekly.

"So how mad are you about everything?" Daryl Junior asks.

Samson's opponent in tonight's match, Tonga, comes down the hall. "Hey, Louie," Samson says. "How you feelin'?"

"Man, you can just put one of them sleeper holds on me tonight. I'm wore out. Had three matches in El Paso and two in Waco in the last five days." Tonga weighs four hundred pounds. Everybody has to back up against the wall to let him get past.

"So do you... like... hate my guts now?" Daryl Junior asks.

Samson looks at him. Daryl Junior glares back, his head trembling slightly.

"So? Do ya?"

"Don't talk crazy. I don't hate you, and I ain't mad. I'm just—"

"Shit, Dad." He turns his back to Samson. "I know you are."

"No... I—"
"Shit."
"I love you, Daryl Junior."
"Shit."

TWENTY-NINE

THE WINNER

In a Texas Cage Death Match, the opponents fight inside a ring around which high walls of wire caging have been constructed. The door of the cage is padlocked, and the match has no time limit. A doctor stands next to the ring throughout the bout and is the one who declares the bout finished. There is no referee.

Tonight's doctor is a little guy wearing a bow tie. He holds his black bag and is accompanied by a uniformed nurse whose hooters look like torpedoes and by an ambulance crew, three men in white.

Inevitably, at the end of a Texas Cage Death Match, the loser is carried off on a stretcher, his face and torso dripping a concoction of cherry Kool-Aide and tomato paste. The ambulance crew rushes him to the life squad that waits outside the arena. The doctor follows. But the nurse always stays behind to attend to the injuries of the winner. She often has him sit on a stool, and she hugs his face to her hooters while she examines his wounded skull, or she instructs him to lie down on the floor of the ring, and she bends at the waist above him, her tight skirt worth at least half the price of admission.

In a Texas Cage Death Match in 1959, The Sheik, who had made a comeback in '57, was brutally punched, kicked, bitten, and pinched by Harry Heavenly for forty-seven minutes before being carried away, his robes blood soaked, by the ambulance crew, a dozen shrieking wives following—and was never seen again. In 1960 *Goliath* magazine reported that he had been rendered impotent, was permanently paralyzed, and was living in seclusion in Cairo, Egypt, with his 366 frustrated wives.

Tonga The African Wild Man enters the cage first. He has yellow stripes painted on his face. On his womanly tits are red X's, and down the center of his huge belly—twice as big as Samson's—is a thick vertical line of green. Although he's so massive that he can barely move, he wears nothing but a loincloth.

"The most merciless wrestler in the world... ," the announcer declares, "weighing four hundred and six pounds... a self-proclaimed cannibal... ladies and gentlemen, I give you... Tonga! The African Wild Man!"

The arena vibrates with boos and hisses.

Samson comes down the center aisle as he's introduced as "Samson The Strong Man! Former world champion! The strongest man in the world! A foreign relations advisor to President Kennedy!"

As Samson approaches the enclosed ring, Tonga throws himself against the caging, screaming and clawing to get at him. The doctor shouts at Tonga, threatens him with a hypodermic needle, until Tonga backs off. Then Tonga and Samson glare at each other through the wire, the one waving the jawbone of an ass, the other an African head-hunter's spear. Tonga lets out more piercing screams. The doctor takes away Samson's jaw bone, then enters the cage and clubs Tonga with it until Tonga gives up his spear. The doctor comes out of the cage to tremendous applause. He straightens his bow tie and bows. His nurse kisses his cheek.

Empty handed now, the two wrestlers glare at each other through the wire some more, waving their fists. Samson The Strong Man shouts, "You gonna pay, Wild Man, for what you done to Buffalo Bill Branson."

The fans who have kept up with events in The World Wrestling Association send up a blood-thirsty cheer. Samson thinks he hears a woman shouting, "I want him dead! Dead! I want the mother fucker dead!"

In a wheelchair, Buffalo Bill makes a timely entrance, rolling down the center aisle. Bill is wearing a neck brace and sunglasses (he is blind from Tonga sticking darts in his eyeballs).

Tonga yells, "Ou ga buga bu!" and lets out a mad scream. He puts his fingers through the cage and bites at the wire (eyeing the nurse's torpedo-like hooters, Samson notices) and makes more animal noises—he wants to finish Buffalo Bill off and have him as a midnight snack.

The doctor takes hold of a microphone that has dropped from the rafters and pronounces, "Let the bout begin!"

Samson opens the door of the cage and charges at Tonga, grabs him by the shoulders, and throws him to the canvas. The crash of Tonga's body reverberates throughout the arena. Now that the bout has begun, the doctor puts a large padlock on the cage door so that neither man can escape.

For most of the match, Samson is backed against the caging, trapped by Tonga's belly and getting whipped up on pretty badly, while the crowd of cowboys and sailors and sluts and fat women and retarded-looking kids scream for Tonga's blood. Samson spots Daryl Junior and Mary about six rows back. When he slips a blood capsule from the pocket of his vest and bites down on it, he hopes it doesn't make Mary sick.

It's hard to keep his mind on his job, and he keeps getting clipped by Tonga's punches. Tonga mutters, "Hey, pay attention. Watch where you's puttin' yo chin." Samson is working on a plan. He can join the Big Time Wrestling Association based in Michigan. He was offered a job there in 1955, and if they still want him, there will be no more putting up with Hoffman. He will move Rachel Marie and the boys and Mary and his grandbaby up there to Detroit.

But as soon as he thinks the word "Detroit," he sees smokestacks and soot-blackened skyscrapers. Snow drifts twenty feet high. Gray skies every day. Rude policemen. Meanest people in the world live up North. He'd be wrestling in Chicago and Gary, Indiana, in Cleveland and Columbus, in Toledo. Lord, it would be like living in a cold Hell. Texas towns are friendly and blue-skied, safe. At least, in comparison.

And what about Candy and Darlene and Tina Lee and the baby in Darlene's belly?

Could he abandon them?

He could send them money in envelopes with no return address.

But he quickly goes on to imagine Candy and Darlene riding up to his house in Detroit in Hoffman's car, getting out, wading through soot-blackened snow drifts to claw his eyes out, Hoffman sitting in his car laughing his head off, Rachel Marie having a heart attack, Daryl Junior sucking on a Camel and blowing smoke in his daddy's face, red holes where Samson's eyeballs used to be.

Samson doesn't hear the shouts and jeers of the crowd or feel the pain in his lips and gums where he's been punched. He is thinking about all the people he loves—his boys, Rachel Marie, Mama, Jean Anne, Ray, Candy, Darlene, Tina Lee, and that baby inside Darlene. Also squeezed into his heart is his grandbaby. Oh, Lord, his heart is bursting.

"Make a show of it," Tonga keeps muttering. "It's 'bout time you cleaned my greens."

He reckons he'll have to do the bouts in Mexico. Screw sheep or pigs—whatever Hoffman has in mind.

Samson sags with sadness, leans into a punch that sends him down—for real. He lies on his face, motionless. Tonga gasps, is so shocked and upset he's about to mess his loincloth.

"Git up! Git up!" Tonga hisses from the corner of his mouth, as he waddles around the cage with his arms raised like a victor. "Git up, you son of a bitch, and clean my greens."

The doctor and the nurse stare into the cage, baffled. Then the doctor looks out into the arena at Buffalo Bill Branson, who just sits in his wheelchair and shrugs. The crowd is booing, their disgust at Tonga's apparent victory deafening. Tonga throws himself on Samson as if he wants to eat him, bites Samson's shoulder, giving everybody more time to figure something out. The doctor fumbles with the padlock, finally removes it from the door, enters the ring, and hops up and down, near the two wrestlers, yelling, "Break! Break!" Tonga knocks him down, and the doctor, with much relief, lies unconscious.

Samson opens his eyes slowly. It felt good to be out. No pain. No worries. Silence. The music of angels. The peace of death.

Now he hears a jumble of voices. The fans are furious. The nurse is screaming like a girl in a horror movie who has just witnessed Martians eating somebody's brain. Then one voice from the crowd is louder than the others: "You sorry sack of shit!"

He sees the blurry face of a crazy-looking Negro. He sees white teeth and the glitter of gold fillings. "Get up and clean my greens, man."

Samson is thinking about all the women and all the children and the mama he loves. And Jean Anne and Ray— God, he wishes they didn't hate him. Their images float in front of him along with the sweaty, contorted, painted face of the giant Negro.

"I love you," Samson says.

"What? What you say?"

Then Samson understands. The fans are screaming. He has a job to do. He has three families to support.

Quickly, he is up, behind Tonga, and has his arms wrapped around Tonga's chest. It's like hugging a bunch of pillows. He squeezes, still thinking about all the people he loves, knowing he isn't going to stop loving anybody, isn't going to be able to change too fast, maybe never. It will go on. He will be sixty, and Candy will be there in Dallas, his wife. Yes, his wife. Darlene in Oklahoma City. More children will come. And he will love them. Grandchildren, too. He will do hideous things in Mexico to save it all. He feels like crying. He just *has* to buy Rachel Marie a dishwasher.

The fans yell, "Kill him! Kill him!" And he squeezes Tonga. It's Samson's famous bear hug. The love hug of death.

"Oh, Jesus!" he calls, as if he were Bible Bob.

God will continue to punish him if he does not change.

"Oh, Jesus," he groans, his heart bursting.

"Oh, my Jesus," he mutters, as he crushes Tonga, and the doctor regains consciousness to declare him, Samson The Strong Man, the winner.

EPILOGUE

EL DOCTOR DE LA MUERTE

Mexico, 1970

The road to Tempoal, Mexico, winds up a mountain— is a long uphill struggle full of blind curves.

Samson's 1957 Studebaker sputters and rattles. The engine whines, and he shifts down. Heat and dust float through the windows and cover the seats and the dashboard and Samson himself. He wistfully thinks of the last Cadillac he owned, his 1962 Eldorado. Instead of getting a new one in '63, he kept it until '64, then traded it in for a '60 Mercury Comet and a few hundred dollars he desperately needed.

In '64 Darlene divorced him, and he wanted no investigations into his finances, so he gave her everything she asked for. When she first announced that she was dead serious about a divorce, he plotted to murder her. He was going to chop her up into little pieces and feed them to the garbage disposal he had had installed when they moved from the trailer park to a subdivision of tract houses. He bought a hatchet and a couple of saws from Sears, Roebuck. But he still loved her, even after all the pain she had inflicted on him. At least now she's remarried to an insurance agent (has been since '66), so he doesn't have to pay her alimony anymore.

About once a month he gets up to Oklahoma City to see Tina Lee and Irving. He takes them toys, and they go to playgrounds and movie theaters (Tina Lee likes the Disney cartoon classics like *Cinderella*, but Irving likes John Wayne and Clint Eastwood westerns and James Bond). Named after Darlene's daddy, who was killed in World War Two, Irving is seven now. Samson thinks "Irving" is a sissy name, but the boy is another Benny Bob, big-boned and strong; Irving has magazine photos of wrestlers all over his bedroom walls: Iron Man Mike, Ed The Eighth Wonder, The Green Beret, Mark Steel, Bobby Shine, Bonito Martinez, and an old photo that Samson had blown up to poster size of Samson The Strong Man in 1955 (the world champion, plenty of hair, a body like Mr. America—hell, like Mr. Universe!).

A truck full of chicken crates passes close on a narrow stretch and nearly runs Samson off the road. He has a good view—a terrifying view—of the valley far below. His breath comes fast; his chest aches. His knees hurt. His back. His feet. He catches a glimpse of himself in the rearview mirror. He looks like a monk, no hair on top, just a fringe around the sides, long enough to cover his ears. His hair would all be gray if he didn't color it a reddish brown. Deep lines crease his forehead.

He looks at his watch, knows he needs to make better time. His bout in Tempoal today is one he doesn't want to miss. It could mean a comeback of immense proportions. A comeback at the age of fifty-one seems unlikely, but Hoffman has given him a new act to try today and has matched him with Bonito Martinez, the Mexican world champion. And Samson is supposed to win, to give Martinez his first defeat ever. It's supposed to be a huge upset. But it's only an exhibition bout, so Martinez won't lose the title. Still, Samson got pretty excited when Hoffman told him the plan.

Martinez wears a mask, and no one knows his true identity. Many people believe he is Bobby Shine, retired now from the CIA or back from a secret space mission.

Some people believe that Bobby Shine faked his death in 1954 merely so that he could safely carry on a secret affair with Lana Turner, but now the affair is over because Lana has lost her looks.

The Studebaker's engine chokes, almost stalls. Samson pumps the gas pedal, coughs on the red dust that fills the car. He's had this car for three years. If things work out today—if there's a positive crowd-response to his new act, his new self—maybe he'll start getting more bouts. Maybe he'll get to drive another Cadillac before he dies.

In '65 Hoffman started cutting back on the number of bouts Samson fought, especially in The States. Although Rachel Marie thinks he still wrestles in Oklahoma City and Dallas, he now wrestles only in Mexico, two or three times a week, still doing The Masked Demon—until today.

The Studebaker continues to cough and sputter. The heat gauge rises. Lord, it would be wonderful to have a Cadillac again. Even the Mercury Comet was better than this.

He let Candy have the Comet when she took off to San Francisco in '67. They never did get married, and now Samson wishes they had. If they had, she couldn't have left him so easily. She started dressing like a hippie and started having hippie friends over to the house so that they could all eat peyote, smoke reefers, and talk bad about the government. He arrived in Dallas one afternoon in the spring of '67 and found her high on marijuana. Some long-haired, bearded guy who looked like the bronze Jesus hanging over their bed was painting daisies on her breasts. Samson broke the hippie's jaw, then drove him to the emergency room. When Samson returned home from the hospital, Candy was packed and said she needed to find a man who practiced nonviolent protest. She muttered something about his age and "the generation gap" and "flower power."

Samson cried and begged her to stay. After he realized he couldn't change her mind, he told her to take the Comet and gave her all the cash he had. She smoked another joint, turned sweet, kissed him, and told him that she would always love him and might even discover she couldn't live without him and come back. He keeps paying the rent on the little red-brick house in case she does return he is almost certain that some day she will need him again. He checks on the house whenever he passes through Dallas. On the kitchen table is a note: "I love you Candy, welcome home." The paper is yellowing; it's covered with dust. Next to it is a fifty-dollar bill, also covered with dust.

Last month, when he visited Tina Lee (who's a cute little thing and is going to be a real heart breaker for sure) and Irving, Samson noticed that Darlene had gained a ton in her butt and thighs and was drinking more than ever. She told Samson at the kitchen table while she put away a six pack of Budweiser that she thought Doug, her insurance-agent husband, was screwing his skinny-ass nineteen-year-old secretary. Her graying hair had fallen into her chunky face, and she kept picking boogers out of her nose. Samson has gotten over her. He doesn't know, doesn't understand where his love for her went, but it's long gone without a trace. He feels only pity for her now.

He stops in Donie when he can. Mama is spry as ever but lonely since Jean Anne died last spring of a heart attack. Jean Anne had gotten moodier and moodier. The night before she died, she and Mama had a fight about who washed the dishes more often and who dirtied more of them. For three days Mama thought Jean Anne was just sulking in her room. Jean Anne had locked herself up a few times before, for a day or two. She'd pee into a pan she had in her room and empty it out her window.

For three days, the door stayed locked. Jean Anne would not answer Mama's pleas for a truce. Mama could hear Jean Anne's TV and knew that Jean Anne hoarded Hostess cupcakes and Twinkies in her room, so she wasn't worried about her starving. Then on the fourth day, a strange and awful smell wafted out from under the door.

Samson cries whenever he thinks about his poor sad sister. In a way, it's his fault. If he had bought Mama a dishwasher....

At least Ray is doing better. Samson paid to send him to a drying-out center five years ago where he met his wife, Mabel, a homely woman a couple of years older than Ray. Ray has found God again, and his bowling scores have improved. He and Mabel manage a motel in Wichita Falls, and Ray takes the youth group from their church bowling every Saturday night. He passes out leaflets on the streets: "Don't do dope! Bowl instead!"; "Bowling, not booze!" Although he is worried about the youth of America, Ray is happier than he's ever been, Samson believes.

A bus comes swaying down the mountain, and Samson pulls over as far as he can. He coughs again, choking on the dust. His head starts to ache. He belches, tastes the tacos he ate hours ago. He does love Mexican food. Mexico could have been a lot worse. Samson has had to wrestle some burros and some hogs, and he's had witch doctors in some of the smaller and more remote towns come to bouts and throw ground-up bones and other magic potions on The Masked Demon. He did, once, back in the fall of '62, have to wrestle a baby bull, naked. But generally the job down here hasn't been as bad as he feared. He got sick from the water only three or four times until he started hauling cases of Dr Pepper around with him. And although he's hurting for money, the lighter schedules of recent years have given him more time with his grandbaby, Rachel.

Daryl Junior's little bride, Mary, lives with Samson and Rachel Marie and Earl and Benny Bob. Little Rachel is six, almost seven, a tiny thing with blonde curls. Samson bounces her on his knee and reads kids books to her, and they look at the pictures in *Goliath* together. She laughs at the pictures and says the wrestlers are funny and scary. Mary helps around the house a lot, especially now that Rachel Marie has bad arthritis. Earl and Benny Bob are driving and have girl friends. They're clean-cut boys, thank the Lord. Earl thinks he might want to be a minister. Benny Bob is a football star, plans to play in college, and should even get scholarship offers.

Daryl Junior is in prison for stealing auto parts from a junk yard.

Although Mexico has turned out better than he expected, he did get lonesome down here, especially after losing Darlene and then Candy. In the late summer of '67— "the summer of love," all the hippies called it—he married Juanita. She's thirty-two, a soft brown woman. She's not a beauty like Candy; her face is too round, her skin a bit coarse, her thighs and waist too thick, and her breasts too small. But she's a good woman who has had a hard life and needs someone like Samson to take care of her.

Before Samson saved her, she was a maid at a hotel where he frequently stayed in Mexico City. He would let her come into his room and clean while he sat in a chair in a corner and played solitaire. He was surprised that she spoke English. Not long after Candy left him, he asked Juanita about herself.

Her husband was killed at a neighborhood cock fight by a razor-clawed rooster that went berserk and leaped into the crowd after its opponent had neatly scooped out one of its eyes. Juanita's husband had his jugular slashed. His blood-drained corpse was hauled off to his house, dumped onto Juanita's kitchen table, and down the street, the cock fights resumed.

Her father had been an English teacher in a small town. "A lover of books," Juanita called him, but a time came when the townspeople decided they didn't need to be paying an English teacher, and he had to make a living from then on by working a variety of jobs. One way he made money was to catch stray animals and sell them to the town's dog-food factory. He had always been gentle with all the family pets, but now he would chase dogs and cats and choke them with his bare hands, then trundle their corpses around in a wheel barrow. He missed teaching; he missed his students. And as he grew older, he lost his mind. He began to believe the stray animals (and not all of them were really stray) were murderers, and he forgot his real purpose, which was to sell them to the dog-food factory. He carried rope with him and hanged the desperadoes. He hanged dogs, cats, goats, sheep, jack rabbits, armadillos, chickens, and hogs. All over town one day, dead animals swung from nearly every tree, and her papa was finally put away.

All big public events in Tempoal are held in the town's church. The priest even allows television cameras in to record the wrestling bouts for replay all over Mexico. Samson has heard that the priest jokes that opening his church to wrestling is the only way to get certain people inside it. In addition, the World Wrestling Association makes a generous contribution to the church's coffers. The priest wears new robes. The local nuns have new habits.

The ring is set up in the front of the church, and the fans sit on both the first-floor pews and in the second-floor balconies.

When Samson arrives, he gets bad news from the referee, Richardo. Bonito Martinez has the flu and can't wrestle. A replacement is on his way from Guanajuato.

So much for another Cadillac.

So much for anything.

Samson sits down in a pew in the back of the church and doesn't think he can get up, is too depressed now to perform tonight. He just wants to sit and cry. He stares at the stained-glass windows that depict Mother Mary with baby Jesus, Jesus surrounded by sheep, and the head of John The Baptist on a platter.

But Samson has a job to do. He has four boys and a girl and a grandbaby to support. He has Rachel Marie to take care of and Mary. And Juanita. Sweet Juanita. She murmurs

Spanish words when he makes love to her. "Muy grande," she says. "Muy grande."

In a small room that priests get dressed in, Samson allows the referee, Richardo, to paint red Valentine hearts of various sizes all over his body. Big ones on his torso. Little ones on his face. A few even on his bald head. All he wears is a pair of red trunks. It is February 14th, and Samson is a new wrestler on the Mexican circuit: Senor Valentino.

He thought his new act would be his rebirth, but he doesn't care anymore. Then looking at himself in the mirror in the little dressing room, he thinks he starts to understand Hoffman's plan.

He hears the ring announcer introduce him. His weight is given in kilos and sounds a lot better than 336 pounds. When he enters the ring, he does understand Hoffman's plan. The nasty, round-faced, pock-marked Mexicans are howling their heads off. He is a joke.

His winning tonight will be a joke, won't mean a thing, wouldn't have even if Martinez had been here. Everyone would have said not only that it was merely an exhibition bout and a non-title bout but that Martinez simply couldn't stop laughing long enough to wrestle seriously.

A 336-pound man covered with hearts. A Cupid with a gland problem.

Samson's head is light. He feels dizzy. He feels a numbness in his left arm.

Bells.

Bells are ringing.

He shakes his head, then realizes that the bout has begun, and for the first time he notices his opponent, a figure in a white smock with a black hood over his head. Samson has never seen this guy before, although he has heard quite a bit about him lately—a future champion, everyone says. But Samson has trouble remembering exactly what the guy's name is. What did the ring announcer call him? Doctor something.

Yes. Doctor....

El Doctor de la Muerte.

El Doctor grasps Samson with large, cold hands and throws him to the canvas and kicks his side repeatedly with a black wing-tipped shoe. The crowd laughs at the way Valentino's belly jiggles, making the painted hearts look as though they were floating on waves.

Samson stays down longer than he should. The gold chandeliers hanging far above him seem to sway. The colors of the painted glass windows blur together. El Doctor de la Muerte keeps kicking. This guy never gets tired.

Samson thinks about cutting the match short—going ahead right now and using the sweet-dream sleeper hold that puts a smile on the loser's face. Then he can get out of here. He will drive through the night to get home to Rachel, Mary, Earl, Benny Bob, and Rachel Marie. Lord, he misses them fiercely.

He rolls over, stands, wobbles, and lunges at the doctor, who sidesteps the attack. As Samson falls, he gets a glimpse of his opponent. The black hood seems to have no eye holes. But that can't be.

Lying face down, he tries to push himself up, but his arms buckle, his face slams into the canvas. He rolls over onto his back and groans.

Pain shoots up his left arm and across his chest, and a light explodes in his head. He can't breathe. Richardo and El Doctor hover over him. Spanish words sizzle in the air just above his chest.

He is dying, he calmly realizes. He is certain he is dying.

And as he dies, he has a vision of Candy being screwed by a skinny-assed hippie. Then he sees Rachel Marie's gray hair and swollen knuckles. Sees Juanita's big brown sad eyes. Sees Mama's smile and each tiny line around her old mouth.

He hears Jean Anne's voice as it was when she was a child say, "I love you, brother."

He feels on his nose and neck and cheeks his children's kisses.

The buzzing of the crowd, a bunch of locusts, is diminishing.

"Jesus," he thinks he says, but isn't sure. All is darkness. "Jesus."

Then a pinpoint of light appears, grows, comes toward him slowly. Jesus is here. At last. To save him.

He hears Jean Anne's voice again. "Love you, brother." The light is brighter. He can barely hear the buzz of the crowd now.

What will his women and children do without him?

"Come, brother," Jean Anne says.

Then silence.

Sweet silence.

Pure, lovely silence—the music of angels.